RIGHT ACROSS THE BAY

QUINN AVERY

For our friends across the bay.
You were right, I'm always watching.

CHAPTER 1
PRESENT DAY

Maxine

I stare in equal parts disbelief and horror as two sheriff's deputies lift the bodybag containing the remains of my lifelong best friend. This can't be real. It can't be happening.

Britta can't be dead.

Oliver, her husband, stands a few feet from her body, his face an ashen mask that doesn't give any emotions away. The attractive med student with an easygoing smile I met decades ago has become hard and arrogant from too many hours standing above an operating table.

He had only been around to witness the discovery

of Britta's body because I'd begged him to come back after she'd been missing for three entire days. I thought it was ridiculous that he hadn't felt the slightest obligation to fly his private plane down the moment I'd first told him her whereabouts were unaccounted for.

The deputies open the back door of the sleek white hearse parked at the edge of the pristine lot, preparing to set the black bag inside. My heart gives a sporadic squeeze.

The macabre scene sharply contrasts with the backdrop of the serene lake, glittering like a thousand precious gems in the morning sunlight. The grand mansion my husband built stretches high into the cloudless blue sky across the bay, framed by hundred-year-old oak trees.

Once again, tragedy will overshadow my life. I had finally experienced a deep, inner peace after moving in with Noah beside the 3,500-acre lake in southwestern Minnesota. Sorrow slashes through my stomach like razor blades. This morning's nightmare will have a lasting impact on our surroundings.

"Maxine!" A warm hand briefly presses against my spine before I'm enveloped in Gabby's signature lilac-scented perfume. "Oh my god, Max, sweetheart, I came as soon as I heard!" She pulls me into an embrace, squeezing her arms until I'm unable to breathe.

"I can't believe she's gone," I rasp against her shoulder.

Just weeks after I moved in, Gabby, a recent widow, came to inspect the modern ranch-style home she'd inherited next door to Noah. After I introduced her to Britta, the three of us formed a tightly knit bond. By the end of that summer, Gabby sold her home in Palm Springs and became a permanent neighbor.

Britta declared us to be the "Fake Housewives of Lake Shetek." She was essentially living independently because of her empire, Gabby's late husband had left her with millions, and I had married into a sizable amount of wealth. It was a ridiculous title, but it was also the kind of outlandish notion that Britta was known to create.

"I'm so sorry." Gabby backs away, smoothing her hand over my dark hair. "I know how much you loved your cousin, and what she meant to you."

Vivid life experiences with Britta—starting with a childhood bond that only first cousins could share—flicker through my mind with the painful rush of a train on a runaway track. *Riding bikes for miles... stealing veggies from our grandmother's garden...fishing for bullheads at the dam...giggling late into the night...*

*supporting each other as our careers dipped and soared…
then finally becoming neighbors for what we thought
would be the rest of our lives…*

"You're my *ride-or-die*," she told me countless
times, usually with a playful spark set deep inside
her bright, cornflower blue eyes.

Although people often commented how we could
pass as sisters, Britta's golden-blond hair versus my
brown, and her wide, expressive eyes set us apart.
Plus my figure could be considered average while
hers was molded to perfection.

Britta built an empire helping women transform
their bodies. Before the era of "influencers," she rose
to fame with her collection of exercise DVDs. Once
her only child left for college, she decided to move
out of Minneapolis and create streaming videos in
the privacy of her home. She built a lakefront
mansion on the land she inherited from our
grandma.

As I watch a deputy close the back door to the
hearse, Gabby's wide hazel eyes, surrounded by a
nest of lash extensions, narrow on Oliver. "He sure
doesn't look too upset. He just seems…*pissed*. He's
probably upset that Brit left him first and now he has
to take care of her."

Take care of her, I think with a deep shiver. *Like she's
a piece of discarded trash.*

The eggs and toast I'd consumed mere minutes before spotting the flicker of red and blue lights across the bay threaten to return. Britta believed in reincarnation. With every new gimmick to come out —*Have your ashes made into a record! Come back in another life as a tree!*—she'd change her mind on what she wanted done with her remains.

Knowing Oliver, he'll simply throw her in a casket and bury her inside a traditional vault. I don't imagine he'll arrange anything beyond a simple grave-side service.

Gabby's perfume clogs my throat when it dawns on me that I'll never again lay eyes on my beautiful cousin's crooked smile, hear her jaded giggle, or experience the comfort of her strong hugs.

"I'm gonna be sick," I declare, pushing away from her. I hustle to the nearest tree, leaning against its bark and dabbing my fingers against my sticky forehead. My stomach violently twists and folds over itself but refuses to give up its contents. I attempt to take deep, calming breaths, but it's as if my lungs have forgotten their job.

A part of me has died along with my little cousin.

It's worse than missing a limb.

I want to disappear along with her.

I would give anything to wake from this nightmare.

Gabby soon stands beside me again, her enhanced lips screwing into a thoughtful expression. "There's nothing more you can do for Brit here. Why don't you come back to my place? You need to get off your feet, have a drink. You can share stories about your cousin, or we can simply get blitzed out of our minds off champagne the way she would want us to. You can stay as long as you want since Noah isn't home."

Wiping at my wet face, I gulp down another cry. "I have to call him. He's in a meeting with clients from Japan…in New York. He doesn't know."

My breath catches.

Oh, god.

New York.

Mention of the city reminds me of Britta's pride and joy, my goddaughter. Taylor remained in New York after graduating N.Y.U. and is engaged to a classmate she met her freshman year. My heart all but shatters when I envision her walking down the aisle without her beloved mother at her side.

"Taylor," I whisper. "I can't leave. She'll need me."

Gabby shakes her head, tossing her white-blond waves around her broad shoulders. "She probably won't arrive until late this afternoon at the very earliest. You can call her after we get to my place." She glances over to where Oliver converses with the sheriff, arms folded and expression grim. "Besides, I'm sure her *doting* father will take care of everything."

At that ludicrous notion, we both burst out in giggles. My laughter is harsh from crying and accompanied by snot. As always, Gabby's is bright and bubbly, causing me to laugh even harder. It's inappropriate to laugh with Britta's corpse nearby, but I suspect it's fueled by a touch of hysteria.

When I catch Oliver scowling our way, I straighten and press my lips together.

"Lets get the hell outta here before *the principal* comes this way to give us detention," Gabby tells me, speaking from the side of her mouth.

As she guides me by my arm toward her black BMW parked on the gravel road, everything about the moment takes on a surreal slant. Dark, forbidding thoughts hover at the edge of my mind.

Britta struggling for air as water fills her lungs.

Waving her hands around her head.

Desperately kicking her legs.

The light leaving her eyes.

With a shiver, I shake my head repeatedly. "I can't believe they found her in the lake. Britta avoided swimming in there at all costs."

Gabby's hazel green eyes flip back towards

Oliver, becoming stern. The faint lines around her full lips deepen with a snarl. "I know."

With her sour expression, I wonder if she's right to imply Oliver may have done something to his wife. Britta's net worth had long since surpassed his generous surgeon's salary, and he wasn't interested in maintaining a healthy marriage any longer.

Then I remember how hard I had to plead with him to come here. When I first realized something was amiss, he had been in Minneapolis—or so he claimed.

The reality that my cousin, my best friend, was possibly murdered causes my stomach to plummet with the force of the first drop on a steep roller coaster ride.

But if Oliver didn't kill her, then who else wanted her dead?

CHAPTER 2
24 MONTHS EARLIER

Maxine

A glass of sparkling wine in hand, I take in the shadowed surroundings from behind the fire pit with a contented sigh. When I moved to Lake Shetek as a teenager to live with our grandmother, the view offered a serenity I never would have thought possible. Sitting on Britta's deck, the familiar blissful comfort begins to return.

Without the bright lights of the city, the stars in the dark sky shine extraordinarily bright and vivid. The houses across the bay are all dark except for the grandest one, constructed with cedar, narrow bricks, and entire walls of glass.

This morning, the neighborhood gradually came to life with the excited chirp of birds and the gentle lap of waves against the rocks on the shoreline. Although most of the lake's residents have yet to move in for the summer months, many of her neighbors are older and retired, living here year-round. They've been quiet, except for the occasional rumble of a lawnmower throughout the afternoon.

When my cousin called four years ago, saying she was building a house where our grandmother's ancient trailer had been, I thought she was insane. Britta's the type that thrives on the madness of the big city life.

Then her mom, who lives forty minutes north of the lake, was diagnosed with dementia. It ended up being a move of convenience once Britta became my aunt's sole caretaker.

Oliver also believed Britta had lost her mind when she informed him of her latest investment. He went along with it anyway. Between their two exuberant incomes, he has the ability to fly a private plane down to visit her on whatever weekends and extended vacations his demanding schedule allows.

Plus they have a strange agreement, allowing them to live their own lives. I'm convinced they haven't divorced since Taylor left home because

Oliver likes to brag about his successful wife to his colleagues.

"Admit it, Max," Britta sings at my side. "You're glad you finally listened to me and came back to Shetek for a visit."

"It stirs a lot of memories," I admit, even though some are unpleasant. "But the view has sure changed." I point to the grand mansion across from us. "Looks like you're not the only millionaire who has moved into the old neighborhood."

"Thank god for that," she says with a dramatic wink. "Otherwise I would've been forced to buy up all those lots and raze those dreadful trailer homes."

"*Grandma's trailer* gave us some great memories," I remind her. "But I can't believe you gave up your favorite gym and choice of night clubs. What is there to do here besides fish and ride bike?"

"Basically, this." She gestures toward the fire while taking a sip of her wine.

I shake my head, unable to envision my high-maintenance cousin doing nothing beyond relaxing in the middle of nowhere. I wouldn't make it a week without having the ability to order takeout from one of hundreds of restaurants in Chicago. "Where do you go for a cappuccino?"

"My kitchen." She leans back in the Adirondack chair and smooths her long and wavy blond hair around her muscular shoulders. Her wide, blue eyes sparkle in the dark every bit as much as the generous diamonds on her fingers. "I dropped ten K on an espresso machine when I moved here—best investment I've ever made. If I hadn't been so busy catching up on social media this morning, I would've made you one. But just you wait until tomorrow."

I take a moment to admire her beauty. She's gracefully tall with striking eyes and high cheekbones, all traits we share. The strict diet and beauty routines she follows are executed by some of the top nutritionists and estheticians in the country, making her flawless. Her glutes and lats are toned and defined from hardcore dedication to her career. Her narrow waist compares to that of a young girl whose hormones have yet to kick in, and her augmented breasts rival an amateur porn star's. Everything about her is impeccable.

"Still," I say, "you don't miss the hustle of the city? Not even a little bit?"

She laughs in a musical sound. "That way of life was becoming exhausting, Max. All that noise and movement gave me constant migraines. I love how I can walk around the seven mile trail behind my place in the middle of the day and only see wildlife. And whenever I need a fix of my old life, I can be in downtown St. Paul in a handful of hours."

"I thought Oliver kept the penthouse in Minneapolis."

Her smile grows. "Exactly." Giggling, she pats my leg. "We can take the boat out tomorrow afternoon, hang out on the beach. The locals are so friendly and naive, just the way I remember. Maybe we can find you a guy to hook up with!"

Tension fills my jaw. My short experience at the local high school proved the locals to be anything but friendly. *Except for Noah and his family*, I remind myself. "I'm perfectly happy without a man in my life."

"You haven't changed one bit." With another sip of her wine, she sniggers. "You should've become a nun after your divorce. At least that way, you could've had a free place to live while being celibate."

I suck down what's left of my wine, letting the snide comment go. My marriage to Roger didn't last because of more than just my intimacy issues and my refusal to give him the houseful of children he wanted.

The real reason I divorced Roger festers in the air between us.

————

The following afternoon, Britta and I sip on vodka and sodas while knee-deep in the lake's murky waters. We're surround by raucous minors drunk off cheap beer and adults well-past their tolerance. Various water toys and anchored jet skis dot the space behind speedboats and pontoons pushed onto the small patch of sand running along the State Park's dense trees. Several radios blast a chaotic mix of country and rock music, the lyrics and melodies almost inaudible above the din of excited conversation and laughter.

A swim would be a heavenly break from the heat, but I follow Britt's lead. Besides, I don't want any of my intimate parts co-mingling with the little dead bugs floating on the water's surface.

Britta's acknowledged by most of the locals. She throws a friendly wave back but isn't interested in engaging with anyone beyond that until an attractive man swaggers in our direction. It's impossible not to appreciate his toned muscles, lush dark hair cascading down to his ears, a stubble outlining his square jaw, and skin bronzed to a golden hue. Black swim trunks, accented with fine blue lines, nicely cup his firm backside.

A deep rush of pleasure spreads through my core when I imagine being encased in those strong arms. The sensation comes on so unexpectedly that I have to swallow a whimper. I haven't fantasized about a man in forever.

I'm suddenly extremely self-conscious about my body. Although Britta goaded me into becoming loyal to gym down the block from my apartment, my C cups could use improvement. The designer one-piece I'd purchased on a whim before coming to Minnesota feels too plain.

Once the man is a few feet away and our gazes meet, all warmth drains from my face.

"Hi, Noah," Britta sings, her greeting going unnoticed.

I'm suddenly 15 again, gazing into the beautiful brown eyes of the boy who once had my heart.

Memories of the 16-year-old who stood up to my bullies blur with the handsome man before me. I never guessed he'd still be living in the area. He always dreamed of moving to a big city.

Struggling to remain upright, I ask in a trembling voice, "Noah?"

"No way." His eyes shine with nostalgia. "Max? Is it really you?"

I shake my head in disbelief, unable to form any words.

"I can't…after all this time," he sputters, bending to deposit his thermos in the sand. He stands tall, arms spread wide as a bright grin sets on his lips. "Come here, you!"

Despite my reservations, I fall into his strong embrace. My body reacts with appreciation faster than my brain. I almost moan.

"I never thought you'd come back to me," he whispers into my ear, his voice crackling with emotion.

Remorse and regret burn through my cheeks. "Neither did I."

With a final squeeze, he sets me down on the sludgy lake floor and steps back. "You look good, Max. *Damn* good."

I don't know what to do with the bold compliment. I'm unsure how to process my reaction to seeing him again. I want to tell him he looks better than anything I could've imagined. I want to tell him I'm sorry for leaving things like I did.

Britta dramatically slaps her hand over her tan chest. "Oh my god, I totally forgot you two knew each other back in the day!"

"How could you forget?" Noah replies, his tone on the edge of annoyance. "I only met you because of Max."

"You're right." With a "silly me" shake of her head, Britta slides a hand over his bicep in a possessive move. "Noah lives right across the bay from me in that impressive house with the massive windows."

My lips tighten. It's odd she "failed" to mention he lived that close until now, especially after I had specifically commented on his house.

"That's quite the place," I say once I've recovered from the shocking news. Something of the mansion's caliber would be worth several million in the Chicago area. He's done well for himself.

"He does something or other in computer engineering with cyber security," Britta explains, still clinging to his arm. "Don't ask me any specifics because it goes way over my head."

"You stuck to your plan," I say, offering a little smile. "Good for you."

Noah's modest grin does a number on my belly. I can't decide if the connection we made as teenagers is still active or if it's all in my head. "I'd love to give you a tour of my house sometime." His thick eyebrows shoot upward. "How long are you here?"

I balk at his question. Merely engaging in conversation with him is a colossal mistake. We share a complicated history that would be best left in the past. As much as he knows, there's even more I'm not ready to share.

"She's here until Saturday," Britta replies on my behalf, turning into him in a way that brushes the bare skin on the tops of her breasts across his arm. "What do you have going on Friday night?"

"I could do Friday," he decides, still addressing me as if Britta isn't falling all over him. "Do you like sushi?"

"It's my favorite," I admit with an electrifying thrill. Despite the long list of reservations filling my head, a part of me wants to catch up with him.

The brilliant stretch of his lips sends a tsunami-sized rush of tingles down to the soles of my feet. "Then it's settled. I'll have my chef come out and prepare enough for three. We can go for a moonlight cruise in my boat after—"

"As fabulous as your idea sounds," Britta interrupts, pulling away from him to spread her fingers across her chest, "I just remembered I have a deadline to meet by Saturday. I'd work on it sooner, but I promised to spend uninterrupted time with Max while she's here. Why don't you two plan to meet up without me? It would work out perfectly. I wouldn't feel guilty for neglecting her one night if you were together, and I'm sure you have so much catching up to do. I'd only get in the way."

Panic rises in my throat. *I can't be alone with him.* As I open my mouth to protest, she nudges me with a mischievous grin and leans close. "You can't turn him down," she whispers. "I think he really missed you."

"I don't know," I whisper back. "I'm—"

"I'll swing over in my boat around six on Friday, Max," he announces, pausing again until he can catch my eye. "Does that sound alright?"

"Looking forward to it," I manage, my lips twitching from the unsettled nerves wiggling throughout my body.

"Then it's a date. But I hope to see you around again before then. The three of us could meet at Pelican later tonight if you're free." He nods at Britta as if confirming the idea, then throws me a charming wink before retrieving his tumbler. He swaggers down the beach at a leisurely pace, bumping knuckles with several of the drunk minors along the way.

I spin my heels through the wet sand to face Britta head-on. "I can't believe you just handed me off to him."

Sniggering, her eyes flicker to the bright blue sky. "Seriously, Max. It's not like he's a stranger. You two clearly have a history."

"Why isn't he wearing a wedding ring?" I demand. *How is someone like him single?*

"He's been married…a couple of times. But it

never sticks. I think he tends to pick women who aren't right for him."

Hearing Britta share intimate facts about the boy I once cared about more than anyone sends shocks of jealousy to war with my growing panic. "Have you slept with him?"

"Why would you ask such a thing?" she answers, her voice clipped.

"You couldn't stop touching him."

"Well, Noah and I have never been anything more than friends," she insists, tugging at my swimsuit tie behind my neck with one of her flirty little grins. "You two, however, are vibing. It must be some history you share. Not that you've ever told me anything about your love life before." With a huff, she rolls her eyes. "We can meet up with him like he suggested. Pelican Cove is his favorite bar—he's there a bunch in the summertime. If you're still undecided about going out with him on Friday, you can claim you aren't feeling well."

My eyes track Noah as he continues to engage with other beach dwellers. He's changed. The sweet boy I once knew now portrays an air of arrogance in the way he struts.

Most importantly, he's too informed of my past. After everything we went through together, how we left things…

Nothing about coming back to Lake Shetek was wise.

CHAPTER 3
PRESENT DAY

Detective Josephine Kelly

While snuggled beneath my fluffy comforter in my Chaska townhouse, my loyal Australian Shepherd tucked in at my side, the Murray County Sheriff calls.

"Would you be able to assist me in solving a high-profile murder case?"

I first met Sheriff Jaros a few years back when he requested my expertise on the disappearance of an 8-year-old girl who had been abducted from her own backyard. He was nearing retirement age and sometimes bent the laws for the locals, but I appreciated his honesty and determination.

Together, we managed to catch the man responsible for kidnapping and then murdering little Lizzy Tanner. We also ensured the pedophile would spend the rest of his life in prison without parole.

Just moments before, I had been weighing the pros and cons of early retirement. If I'm being honest, however, I take too much pride in maintaining a close to impeccable record. It would be almost impossible to leave it behind. I'm known for having a keen eye and laser-sharp instincts that seldom steer me wrong. I've spent over two decades solving murders in the Midwest.

In that time, I've seen it all. Some of the more grisly things—like the spoiled teenager who had taken an axe to his parents when they had failed to buy the gaming system he wanted or the wife who had tried dissolving her cheating husband's slain body with the wrong type of acid—I wish I could purge from my memory.

My demanding and often exhausting career has made me hesitant to invest in a relationship since finishing the academy. Instead, I adopted Henry from the shelter as a companion. Knowing I'll have to leave him behind if I accept the assignment, I sink my fingers into my sweet dog's thick hair and sigh.

There have been several eligible suitors over the years. I almost agreed to marry a fellow cadet in the academy long before he was fired from his first assigned station for accepting a bribe. And I'm constantly being asked out on dates. I stay in shape, and I'm blessed with big chocolate-colored eyes and a headful of strawberry blond hair. The pistol strapped to my hip also seems to bring out men's secret desires to be dominated.

But my schedule tends to be chaotic, especially as I'm often deputized in other counties to help solve more complicated murders.

Without hesitation, I tell Sheriff Jaros, "I'll be there as soon as possible."

While packing my trusty duffel bag for whatever time I'll be spending on the shores of Lake Shetek, I remind myself it's better to be alone. The hassle of finding someone to watch Henry is distressing enough.

———

Hours later, I take a final look at the pale corpse with a Y-incision over its chest cavity on the medical examiner's table. The victim, aged 40, was in excellent physical shape. Although fish and turtles nibbled at her flesh in the short time her body was submerged beneath the shallow lake, I instantly recognized the fitness instructor.

I had played Britta Baxter's DVD every morning for six straight months after my mother passed away unexpectedly. I needed an outlet for my pent-up energy when dealing with the family drama that followed. Associating the vivacious woman from the video with the lifeless body on the metal table proves disheartening.

Without question, Britta Baxter had been murdered. The medical examiner had explained in detail how she had been stabbed twelve times in the back before drowning. The ligature mark around her ankle was from a rope tied to an anchor in an attempt to keep her submerged.

Fortunately, the wind had picked up the night before, and the body had floated into shallow waters. One of the area residents had spotted her while fishing in a canoe. The murder weapon, however, was still unaccounted for.

"Someone from the B.C.A. will be coming down from St. Paul," Dr. Schreier, the medical examiner, tells me. Her hazel eyes become heavy with sympathy when she glances down on the body. "They'll help identify the type of knife used and write up a profile of the attacker. Unfortunately, it could be another week or two before they're able to fit her in."

My smartphone buzzes against my hip. "Thank

you," I say to the doctor while pulling my phone from its holster. "I'll be in touch."

As I start for the hallway to answer the incoming call, I suddenly wish I hadn't quit smoking two years prior. I could use a shot of nicotine to take the edge off. "Detective Kelly."

"The husband voluntarily came in to see me," Sheriff Jaros's baritone voice replies. "Not sure how long I can keep him here because he said he has a flight to catch, but I think you should talk with him… see if you think he's good for it."

"What does your gut tell you, Sheriff?"

"He could be our man. My deputies are searching the Baxter property and knocking on the neighbors' doors to see if they're missing an anchor. One of my men cut the rope off her ankle before they recovered her body from the water, so no one knows it was used in the murder except us and our perp."

I cringe. While I can appreciate the small community mentality, with murder cases far and few between, the deputy had disturbed substantial evidence. "Did they at least get a picture of the knot before they cut it off?"

The sheriff grunts. "My deputy was too upset about the state of Miss Baxter's body to think it through. You have to remember, Detective, she was a big-time celebrity to the locals. And Deputy Willis is still a bit green behind the ears. He's only been out of the academy for a handful of months."

"You mean *Mrs.* Baxter," I amend.

"Most folks around here forget she's married. The way rumors around here go, I suppose she forgot, too. She made her way around town if you get my drift."

With a dissatisfied grunt, I acknowledge the list of potential suspects is about to grow. "I'm on my way, Sheriff."

———

In a matter of minutes, I've parked outside the brick building in downtown Slayton. I join Sheriff Jaros outside the interrogation room in the heart of the station, passing on the cup of coffee he offers.

I usually avoid judging a potential suspect until I've spoken with them in detail. But upon first seeing Oliver Baxter waiting behind the two-way mirror, I struggle not to label the new widower as an arrogant prick.

Sitting rigid in the plastic chair, he checks the gold Rolex on his left wrist with unrestrained irritation. One would think he was being stood up by a patient rather than mourning the tragic death of his wife.

Judging by the crease of skin around his eyes and

flecks of light gray at the temples of his wavy chestnut hair, I guess him to be between forty-eight and fifty-five. He has the long, lean body of a marathon runner and the remarkably smooth hands expected of a surgeon. With a defined jaw and alluring gray eyes, I suspect he would be rather handsome if he were to smile.

"I've never met the man before today," Sheriff Jaros comments from beside me, "but I'd say he's the classic definition of a narcissist."

Huffing in agreement, I breeze into the room. "Dr. Baxter? I'm Detective Josephine Kelly. I was brought in by Sheriff Jaros to help investigate your wife's death."

His thin upper lip lifts to reveal piano-key-straight teeth bleached bright white. "And you consider me to be a suspect." The deep bass of his voice booms in the small space, clipped with anger.

"At this stage, I'm merely interested in extracting as much information as possible." I sit across from him and rest my folded hands on the table. Since the sheriff was confident no one had seen the stab wounds when the victim was first brought to shore, I decide to test the husband. "Was your wife an avid swimmer?"

His expression darkens. "My wife despised swimming in lakes. She was a pool rat when she lived in Minneapolis but refused to submerge herself in the same space fish defecated." His voice oozes with disdain as he continues, "It's part of the reason I thought she had lost her mind when she announced she was *relocating* to this wasteland."

"You're implying she planned to move here without you. Were you separated at the time?"

"Not officially. We merely had an…arrangement."

"You mean an open marriage?"

"I *mean*, not every marriage functions in the tradi-tional sense. My wife and I were in the same social circle as many couples who choose to reside in sepa-rate homes, and lead separate lives. Sometimes couples are happier that way." His gaze hones onto my left hand. "Are you married, Detective?"

Struggling not to roll my eyes in response, I ignore the question. "What's the benefit of that arrangement?"

"It was never Britta's intention to settle down and start a family. She fell pregnant with our daughter while on antibiotics during her sophomore year of college. I did the noble thing and asked her to marry me. She spent the next decade traveling the country under the guise of promoting her brand, usually with our daughter and nannies in tow. Once Taylor graduated high school and left for N.Y.U., Britta decided her obligation to me had ended."

"Why not get a divorce?" I ask.

His nostrils flare with irritation. "After twenty years, our finances have become deeply intertwined. Instead of spending hundreds of thousands on lawyers and wasting precious time in courtrooms, we decided to proceed with the status quo."

Sounds like quite the love affair. It's another reason to believe I've dodged a bullet by staying single. "I have yet to delve into your wife's financial affairs for myself, but according to a quick search on the internet, her net worth is estimated to be in the tens of millions. That's a substantial amount compared to a surgeon's salary."

"And you think that would be my motive?" He shakes his head, sniggering. "Good try, Detective. My wife set up a trust after our daughter was born, ensuring her empire would pass along to Taylor in this situation. I'll only receive Britta's share of the penthouse we owned in downtown Minneapolis."

"Are you in touch with your daughter?" *Are you close enough to manipulate her into sharing her inheritance?* I really wonder.

"What kind of question is that? I'm her father."

"I'm assuming you've informed her by now that her mother died?"

"Of course. I couldn't tell her in person since her flight arrives late this evening."

My eyebrows lift. Although I've never been close with my family, it must be unusual for a father not to support his child in such a crisis. "You're not sticking around to comfort your grieving daughter?"

"I've already rescheduled three entire days' worth of surgeries. I can't afford to stay in this shithole one minute longer. Taylor's friend is picking up her at the airport and bringing her home. Taylor's godmother will be around to take care of her. Max is like a second mother to Taylor."

Sheriff Jaros had only glossed over the facts of the case on my drive from Chaska to Slayton, but I'm pretty sure the name *Max* had come up before. I make a mental note to ask this Max person about the relationship between the doctor and Taylor. "And who is Max? A family friend?"

"Britta's cousin. She's the one who reported Britta as missing."

I recall the most crucial bit of the conversation I had with the sheriff during my drive. He said Britta's husband didn't so much as flinch when they removed her body from the water. "You don't seem too upset about your wife's death."

"Like I said, we had a marriage of *convenience*," he

snarls with redness blooming across his face. "We hadn't been intimate with each other in years."

"Not with *each other*, but with *others*?" I assume.

"On occasion."

"You were aware your wife was sleeping with other men?"

The doctor jerks his head to the side, glowering at the 2-way mirror with his jaw clenched. "We never discussed the details of what went on when we were apart."

My pulse kicks up a notch. I've finally struck a nerve. "Did it bother you to think she was having sex with someone other than you?"

"Of course it bothered me! She was my wife!"

"Are you aware if she had been sleeping with someone in the days leading up to her death? Is it possible she had a lover who didn't like the fact that she was still married?"

With another shake of his head, he abruptly stands. "I'm going to miss my flight," he snaps, eyes narrowed with a silent threat.

"Just one more question, Dr. Baxter," I say before he can slip from the room. "Where were you on June seventh, the day your wife's cousin called to report her missing?"

The doctor's expression morphs into something much more menacing. "I'll leave my lawyer's name and number with the receptionist at the front desk. You can direct any more questions you may have his way."

With the slam of the door behind him, I utter a "humph" into the empty room. While I'm not convinced the doctor murdered his estranged wife, I'm not about to rule out either him *or* a secret lover.

CHAPTER 4
29 YEARS EARLIER

Noah

After the final bell of the day rings, I blend in with dozens of my classmates eager to head home. Glancing down the hallway, I decide girls are so damn weird. I'm convinced it's a proven fact. There's a book on my mom's nightstand that says something about them being from the planet Venus. It would explain a lot.

The homecoming dance is a week away, and I still don't have a date. I asked a couple of girls from my Earth Science class, neither of them too hard on the eyes, but they both claimed they already had a date.

Three others that I consider to be friends said it would be too weird to think of me as their "date."

I thought finding someone would've been easy since I'm the quarterback and get along with many of my classmates. Guess I was wrong. Then again, girls have never really been on my radar, so maybe I'm just too inexperienced. I've always been more focused on keeping up with schoolwork so I can attend the engineering school of my choice.

It doesn't help when everyone in the school believes the rumor that Tara Harrison and I are a thing. Truth is, I can't tolerate being in the same room as her. She has this long, curly blond hair, and a big chest, so I'll admit she's hot or whatever. But she's too into the popularity thing and wears super short plaid skirts and colorful leggings with low-cut sweaters. She's so not my type.

The firm grip of my best friend, Travis Ingman, clamps down on my shoulder. "Did you see what Tara's wearing today?"

"Tara who?" I ask. Although I know exactly who he's talking about, it's a fair question since there are 300 kids in our high school, including more than one Tara.

"*Tara who*?" he mocks with a snigger, smacking the back of my head. "Dude. We're talking about the smokin' hot girl you're gonna hook up with after the dance next weekend!"

"Not happening," I say, shifting my textbooks to my left side to rub the back of my head with my right. "If you think she's so hot, why don't you ask her to the dance?"

"Because she's destined to be yours, bro. I heard she already has names picked out for your future children."

I snort. "As if."

We pass a group of girls whispering to each other with their hands held to their mouths and funny grins on their lips. This high school is brutal when it comes to bullying. I can't help wondering if all girls are that way or if southwestern Minnesota is extra bad.

All I know is my little sister, a 7th grader, comes home from school almost every day with tears in her eyes.

"Hello, ladies," Travis calls out to the girls. They all giggle in response.

When we reach our lockers, I turn to him as we're both spinning our padlocks. My dad's out of town for a mortuary conference, and my mom signed up for the night shift at the hospital, so I'm without a ride. I enjoyed having the freedom of being home alone when I was younger, but now it's just a major inconvenience.

Living in a community too small for a public bus forces me to either bum a lift from my buddies or hoof it the two miles back home. I wouldn't care, except it's starting to turn brutally cold and dark earlier.

"Can you give me a ride home after practice?" I ask.

Travis tosses his books into his locker while shaking his head. "I would, man, but I promised my old man I'd skip practice to drive the grain cart. It's supposed to rain all weekend, so he wants to harvest the last bit of beans before then."

Sometimes, it can be weird to live in a farming community. During harvest season in the fall, a lot of my buddies are excused from class to help their dads or grandpas in the field. Sometimes, they're even absent for planting season in the spring. Most of them plan to work for their dads right out of school and eventually take over their family's operation.

There's no way I'll be walking in my dad's footsteps and working with dead bodies. I have much bigger plans.

"Have fun with that," I tell him, trying to make light of the situation. Honestly, I wouldn't mind being a farmer's kid. I would gladly accept the use of a rusted-out pickup truck. Several of my friends started driving themselves to school our freshman year.

Travis slugs my shoulder. "Later, bro."

As he's walking away, I chuck my things into my locker and re-engage the lock right as Tara's voice cuts through the hallway.

"Oh, *my god*," she sings, her annoying tone sharp with judgment. "Where did you get that nasty old shirt? Your *grandpa's closet*?"

A chorus of giggles follows.

I glance over my shoulder to witness Tara squaring off with a girl in the middle of the hallway. I've only seen the girl around a few times, so I guess she's either new to the area or in 8th grade.

Hiding behind a mess of long, dark hair, her reaction to Tara's bitchiness is hard to interpret. In an oversized flannel over a T-shirt, ripped jeans, and skater shoes adorned with designs from a permanent marker, she blends in with the other girls—with the exception of Tara and her crew.

At least the girl doesn't appear to be as intimidated by Tara's ridicule as I'd been expecting. She stands in place, seeming to hold her ground.

"Seriously," Tara continues with her group of friends still giggling at her side, "I think you totally need to check that shirt for a bug infestation. It looks like it could have fleas."

Remembering all the times my sister has cried because of bullies, I yell, "That's *enough*!" Once I realize my voice came out exceptionally hard, it's too late. Tara and her friends are giving me looks that could kill. I clear my throat and make my voice soft. "Knock it off, Tara."

With one hand planted on her hip, an ugly scowl spreads over Tara's blood-red lips. I remember Travis's comment on her outfit and realize I haven't taken a second to register what she's wearing. The flash of her pierced belly button beneath a cropped sweater and a skirt short enough to violate the school's policies do nothing for me.

"Oh, I'm sorry," she sneers. "Did I insult your *girlfriend*?"

Doing my best to ignore her, I step closer to the girl and gently nudge her arm. She smells nice, like fabric softener and some kind of flowers. "Let's get outta here."

Hazel eyes with little flecks of gold lock with mine, unmoving. They're cool. But I wonder if she's hard of hearing.

"You don't have to stand here and put up with her shit," I say a little louder. "Come on." I head for the exit at the end of the hallway. A few seconds later,

I hear the sound of the girl's rubber soles shuffling over the cracked linoleum behind me.

"You better think real hard about what you're doing right now, Noah Huisman," Tara calls out behind us. "You're choosing a side, and it's the wrong one."

"So damn dramatic," I mutter when pushing on the door that leads to the courtyard. I hold it open until the girl joins me on the building's front concrete steps. "Sorry about that. I have no idea what her problem is."

I don't know why I'm apologizing on Tara's behalf, except I'm suddenly super nervous when standing close to the girl with pretty brown hair and cool eyes. Jamming my hands into my pockets, I lift one shoulder. "I'm Noah."

"Whatever," she answers with a huff. Her voice is much deeper than I would've expected.

"You don't have to tell me your name. It's just—"

"Max."

Kind of a weird name for a girl. Then again, it seems fitting for her no-b.s. attitude.

The wind picks up, stirring leaves in the yard and blowing Max's hair away from her face. She has high, thick eyebrows the same rich shade of brown as her hair. Her lips look velvety soft, like a set of flower petals. Paired with a button nose and those intense eyes, she kinda reminds me of Cindy Crawford, minus the mole.

I can't believe I haven't *really* noticed her before.

My pits break out in a sweat. "You new here?"

"None of your business, *Noah*." The way she slightly exaggerates her vowels makes me wonder if she's from the south. With a challenging look, she marches down the sidewalk, past the lines of school-mates waiting for their buses.

I jog to catch up with her. "Do you live close by? Can I walk you home?"

"What's your *deal*?" she demands, cranking her head in my direction. "Did you lose a bet, and now you have to hang out with the weird girl?"

The sudden burst of anger straightens my spine. She has every right to be mad after what Tara said, but I had nothing to do with it. "I don't think you're weird."

Her eyes narrow into slits. "Then *you're* the weird one. Aren't you supposed to be one of the popular jocks?"

"Whatever. Labels are dumb."

"*You're* dumb," she says with a deep huff, still walking at a fast clip. "That's what everyone will say if they see you with me."

"Like I'd care." I lift one shoulder. "What's so bad about you?"

"Trust me when I say you don't want to find out."

She breaks into a jog, making it clear she's done talking to me.

I stop to watch her, chuckling to myself. She might be the coolest girl ever.

———

I don't see Max again until the day before the homecoming dance. I gave up trying to find a date after my eighth rejection. Honestly, I no longer care. It's a stupid dance.

But seeing Max breeze down the hallway gives me an idea. She looks way different this time in a long blue dress over a plain white T-shirt. The sides of her dark hair are pulled away from her face in a scrunchie. There's even a little makeup on her eyes and those flower-like lips shine with gloss.

It's jarring how she's even prettier compared to the other day. Someone like her must already have a boyfriend…somewhere.

"Max, wait up!" I holler, nudging my way past a few classmates to join her. "How've you been?"

"Oh, Noah…hi," she replies in a soft, quiet voice. She turns to me with a big, bright smile that makes my gut do a weird little dance. "I'm good. You?"

I try not to laugh. She had been so short with me

the last time we spoke that the friendly attitude takes me by surprise. "Ummm…great. I was wondering…I mean…do you have plans for tomorrow night?"

Her super cool eyes widen. "For the dance?"

"Well, actually, I thought maybe you'd like to do something else with me. You know, do something different. I mean, dances at the school are so lame." The urge to slap my forehead comes out as a quiet grunt. "Unless, of course, you have a boyfriend. Not that I'm asking you out, just wondering if you wanted to hang."

She bites her full bottom lip, rolling her shoulders forward. "I can't. My cousin is coming down from the cities to stay with me at my grandma's for the weekend."

"Bummer." My own shoulders drop with disappointment. Looks like I'll be going solo to the dance after all. Still, I don't want to give up on a chance to get to know this girl. "You could come over another time. My mom is way into movies, so we have this big collection of VCR tapes. We could hang out and watch whatever you want."

Her eyes dart away. "I, uh…" Complexion all at once pale, she shifts her weight. "That isn't a good idea."

Although the shy, uneasy response throws me for a loop, I get the feeling there's a valid reason for her reaction. I wouldn't trust anyone after being a target of Tara and her friends, either.

"If it would make you more comfortable, I could invite my little sister to join us," I tell her. "You'd like Shelly. She'd be better at picking out a movie anyway."

"Maybe." Clutching her books against her chest, she gives my acid Levis and red Nike sweatshirt a glance. The slightest hint of a smile dances in her gaze when our eyes meet. "I'll see you around, Noah Huisman."

I sure hope so, I think with a grin big enough to split my lips.

CHAPTER 5
PRESENT DAY

Beth

When I push through the tall black doors of Club Desire in downtown St. Paul, the energy inside pulsates. I blow a kiss to the bald, stout bouncer. Even though I'm mature enough to skip the ID routine without any hesitation, he recognizes me from our past hook-up. His lustful gaze lingers on my breasts, spillin' from the tight corset intended for that purpose.

The nightclub is unusually busy today, and I'm pleasantly surprised to find so many eligible bachelors starin' at me.

Men are so predictable, it's almost comical.

The incessant thumpin' of hip-hop music comin' from the club's 10-foot speakers is unbearable. I head towards the smaller bar in the far corner, away from the dance floor. Even though I can shake my ass better than women half my age, I prefer to lose myself in the company of an attractive man in private. I get off on toyin' with them.

The bartender, in his 20s, has black dreadlocks, a goatee, and dozens of tattoos. As I sit down, he watches me with interest. After a moment, his dark eyes flicker with recognition. I've been here durin' his shift a handful of times, enough to know how much he enjoys flirtin'. I'm sure he's this way with all female customers. But it's only a matter of time before he begs to get a piece of me. Guys like him always do.

"Hey there, gorgeous," he practically growls. His dark gaze sweeps over the tight corset before settlin' on my eyes. "Haven't seen you in a hot minute."

A flirtatious retort gets caught in my throat as a photo of Britta Baxter appears on the TV above him. A banner below her smilin' face reads, "FITNESS GURU'S BODY FOUND IN SOUTHWESTERN MINNESOTA."

"Turn that up!" I snap, without botherin' to conceal my annoyance.

The bartender shuffles away lookin' confused and

slightly irritated when retrievin' the remote. As the female anchor explains the situation, old videos flicker on the flat television screen.

Britta, in a revealin' ballgown, at a Hollywood premiere…

Britta, in skin-tight workout clothes, demonstratin' a move with a barbell…

Britta, in form-fittin' sweatpants and a hooded sweat-shirt, walkin' to an SUV with a brunette toddler in her arms…

Britta, in a sparklin' princess-style dress, alongside her handsome husband at a charity event…

It's enough to make a girl violently gag.

Women like Britta Baxter feel an innate need to project perfection 24/7, even when their lives are crumblin' around them. Women like her fill little girls with false expectations and force other women to obsess over everythin' that's lackin' in their lives.

Snakes like her exemplify everythin' wrong with society and shine a spotlight on the dangers of social media.

A smile edges across my lips. "That bitch finally got what she deserved."

"You know her?" the bartender asks, scratchin' his cheek with unease as he glances up at the screen.

"You could say we were *well acquainted.*"

I reach into the waistband of my skin-tight

leopard pants and pull out a wad of $100 bills. I peel off one and hand it to him. "You and me are doin' a shot from the most expensive bottle you have. Then I'm takin' you out into the alley so we can have us a *real* party."

There's never been a better reason to celebrate.

CHAPTER 6
PRESENT DAY

Maxine

Sipping on a fresh cup of cappuccino, I stare at our grand home across the bay as the sun rises behind it. A golden glow flashes through the massive bay windows, reflecting onto the still lake. It isn't often I witness the sunrise from Britta's perspective, cast across our yard.

Noah returned my call the night before, several hours after he'd wined and dined his company's potential new clients in the heart of Manhattan. When I told him about Britta, he insisted on taking the next flight home. I assured him I would be too busy consoling Taylor to notice his presence. I suspect he would've secretly resented me if he had canceled his meetings.

When I checked on Taylor early this morning, she was wide awake, curled up on her mother's bed. As she told me she hadn't slept all night, her red-rimmed eyes were nearly swollen shut. Once she was nestled in my arms, she finally passed out.

I felt connected to my cousin in the posh king bed, surrounded by the high-end decor Britta had painstakingly selected to suit her personality. It's the perfect blend of feminine and modern with fluffy white bedding, oversized pillows, a grand walnut bed frame, and soft white drapes hanging alongside the grouping of windows overlooking the lake.

Britta never closed the drapes. I know this for a fact because there was a spot in our master bathroom that allowed an unobstructed view of the foot of her bed.

I'd seen her parading around at night in skimpy lingerie. More than once, I'd caught her engaging in adventurous sex with men who weren't her husband.

My phone buzzes with yet another call from my mother. She's been trying to reach me ever since Britta's death leaked on social media the night before. If I don't speak with her at some point, her calls will only become more frequent. For now, I reject the call and flip my phone around, hiding her condescending face.

An engine roars on the street side of the house. Then there's the unmistakable creak of a metal door. I lean to the side, glancing through the house's interior. Much like the architecture of our home, Britta's is encased with large, over-the-top windows. It provides a clear view of the front step.

An attractive woman in her mid 40s, reddish-blond hair brushing a few inches past her shoulders, waits outside the front doors. From her rigid stance and the black blazer she wears with no-nonsense slacks, I'm convinced she's law enforcement of some kind and not a reporter. So far, only a few have made an appearance since the news of Britta's death went national.

I set my cappuccino on the chair's arm and race back inside before the woman decides to ring the doorbell. Swinging one of the 8-foot doors open with one hand, I smooth my dark hair down with the other. "Can I help you?"

The woman nudges her blazer aside, revealing a gold badge clipped to her waistband. She's naturally beautiful with striking eyes that demand attention. Her makeup-free face remains smooth until a tight smile produces little wrinkles around her eyes.

"Detective Josephine Kelly. I'm sorry to disturb

you, but I understand Dr. and Mrs. Baxter's daughter arrived late last night. I need a few minutes of her time."

"She had a long night. She's finally asleep."

When I press my lips together, the detective's expression softens. "I'm sure she's exhausted. I would let her sleep, but I must speak to her as soon as possible."

"Do you think Britta was…" I swallow the dry lump rising in my throat, refusing to utter the words that will make the truth more tangible. "I mean, was she—"

"We have reason to believe there was foul play involved." Folding her hands against her thighs in a military-like stance, she tilts her head sideways. "I'm sorry. And you are…?"

"Maxine Huisman. Britta's cousin. We're—I mean, we *were*, like sisters."

Understanding crosses her otherwise steely gaze. "Ah, Mrs. Huisman. You live across the bay from here in that stately house with the movie-screen-sized windows. Correct?"

"That's right," I confirm, hugging myself.

"I'm sorry for your loss." A smile tinted with empathy crosses the detective's natural berry-stained lips. "I've been trying to reach you. If it's alright, I would like to ask you a few questions before I speak with Taylor."

"Sure." I drop my arms from around me to pull the door open a little wider. "Let's go out to the back deck so we don't wake Taylor any sooner than necessary. Can I get you something to drink? A water or a soda?" I consider offering to make her a cappuccino, but I didn't realize how much noise the machine made until I'd hit the start button. I don't want to make that mistake again.

"I'm good, but thank you."

The detective follows me into the house and through the double French doors leading to the covered deck. As we settle in the chairs around the teak table, she lets out a low whistle. "I was here yesterday afternoon, but the yard looks different this time of day with the early sunlight. That's some view."

"Britta practically lived out here," I tell her with a wistful smile. "Even in the winter, she hung out beside the fire pit, bundled in a down blanket and a knit hat."

Detective Kelly removes a small recording device from inside her blazer. "Do you mind?"

My shoulders lift with a half-hearted shrug. "I'm willing to do whatever I can to help."

With the press of a button, a red light appears

before she sets the device on the table between us. "How long had you and Britta been close?"

"Since birth. Well, hers. She was four years younger."

"You were first cousins?" she asks.

Twisting my fingers together, I merely confirm with a nod until she points at the machine. "Oh—sorry, yes," I sputter. "Our moms are sisters."

Expecting her to continue with detailed questions about my family and childhood, my heart thuds hard enough to shake my entire body. But she goes in an entirely different direction with, "Did you spend a lot of time together outside of family gatherings?"

Relieved that she's not interested in prying into my background, I let out a shaky breath. "We were maids-of-honor in each other's weddings, and I'm Taylor's godmother. We went on vacation together yearly, sometimes with Taylor and sometimes just the two of us. Before I moved here, she visited me in Chicago as much as our schedules allowed."

"How long have you lived with Mr. Huisman?"

"Almost two years."

She squints, causing deep lines to crease between her eyes. It seems she's a good decade older than I first guessed. "Where did you live before that?"

"I moved to Chicago with my first husband two years after graduating from the U of M. We divorced before our fifth wedding anniversary. I remained in Chicago until I moved in with Noah."

"That was convenient, moving directly across from your cousin."

Irritation slices through me. "What is that supposed to mean?"

She waves both hands through the air as if erasing the comment. "Nothing. Sorry, I just meant it was good fortune to have met a man who lived so close."

"I didn't just meet Noah," I clarify. "We've known each other since high school."

"I see." When she runs her fingers back and forth along her jaw, I notice she isn't wearing a wedding ring. "How long have you known Britta's husband?"

"Long enough. Oliver and my ex-husband were in their third year of med school at the U when I finished my undergraduate degree. We met at a bar downtown."

"What's your overall impression of Dr. Baxter?"

A dry bark of a laugh bursts from my lips. "You're asking if I think he's capable of killing Britta."

She responds with a half-committed shrug. "Do you?"

"Possibly. They stopped having a relationship with each other a long time ago. I wouldn't be surprised if he wanted her out of the picture so he could start over with someone younger. Britta only got into fitness because Oliver expects perfection. After she had Taylor, she panicked and became obsessed with working out. She followed a weird diet that nearly starved her to death. She would never admit it because it would ruin her reputation and credibility, but I know she had several procedures done in the past few years. She'd go weeks without answering my video calls, then she would finally reach out wearing a ton of makeup to hide the bruises."

"What makes you think those bruises weren't the result of abuse?"

"I was an RN in Chicago, spent several years working in the ER. I've seen everything. Besides, she wasn't living with Oliver at the time. And he's obsessed with his work—he would never risk injuring his hands."

"But you think he may have risked it to ensure she was permanently out of his life?"

"I wouldn't rule it out."

"Do you have any reason to believe she was afraid of her husband? Had she ever mentioned any heated arguments…any threats he might've made?"

"No. They didn't spend enough time together to argue."

"What's the relationship like between Dr. Baxter and his daughter?"

"It's civil," I say, shrugging. "They aren't as close as they were when she was little."

"Does she generally listen to what he says...take his advice?"

I release a harsh laugh. "Taylor's as independent as her mother. Not many people can tell her what to do or how to do it."

Detective Kelly leans back, crossing one leg over the other and jiggling a booted foot through the air. "You're the one who reported Britta as missing to the police."

"That's right."

"And that was on June seventh?"

"Yes. We have a standing appointment every Wednesday at her favorite spa in Sioux Falls. She wouldn't have missed that appointment for anything."

"When had you last seen her prior to that day?"

"The night before. Whenever Noah's out of town, which is pretty often, we usually meet up for a glass or two of wine." With the memory of our last moments together, I shiver. "We shared a bottle of Prosecco that night."

"Did you have that bottle here or at your place?"

"Here. On this deck. I think I stayed until a little after eleven."

"Did you drive home?"

"We have a small rowboat that I use to cross the bay whenever it's fairly warm out."

The detective taps a hand against her boot. "Dr. Baxter's lawyer sent the surgical log from the last seven days. He was with patients all day on the sixth and seventh."

A snorting laugh vibrates deep against my throat. "He has his pilot's license and shares ownership of a small commuter plane with three other men. He could've easily flown down here for a few hours and returned for surgery the next morning. You should ask his lawyer to send a log of *that*."

She stands and pushes her hands into her back pockets while gazing across the lake. "You can see pretty clearly into your house from here. I imagine when Britta's lights were on, you had a clear view of everything that went on inside her house."

"Sure, but I tried not to spy on my cousin."

"Did you notice anything strange after you left here that night? Maybe her lights stayed on longer, or you saw movement within the house?"

"I was tired that night…passed out as soon as I got home."

The detective's eyes narrow. "Can you think of

anyone who may have been angry with your cousin, who would've wanted to do her harm? An old business acquaintance…a delusional fan…maybe a scorned lover?"

"Britta was a beloved celebrity. Everyone worshiped her."

"Including you?"

"Of course!" I snap. "I loved her like a sister!"

She tilts her head with a borderline condescending smile. "You never had any reason to fight? Any jealousy towards her success?"

"I don't appreciate what you're implying," I reply through clenched teeth.

With a slight nod, she retrieves the recorder and slips me a business card from inside her blazer pocket. "Thank you for your time, Mrs. Huisman. If you can think of anything that may be relevant to my investigation, no matter how small, please reach out. That's my personal cell number on the bottom."

"You better find the monster responsible for taking my cousin from me, Detective," I say, running my fingers back and forth over the letters embossed on her card. "She didn't deserve this."

Her sharp eyes remain on mine when she nods. "Oh, you can bet I'll find her killer."

CHAPTER 7
29 YEARS EARLIER

Noah

After inviting Max to my house, she started coming by at least once weekly over the next several months. Shelly was instantly drawn to her. The two formed a close friendship over their love of grunge music and Max's willingness to let Shelly experiment with her hair. I was first a little jealous. Then I realized they were both loners and needed each other.

Besides, the more time I spend around Max, the less I want to be her friend. I've been itching to ask her on an official date, but Shelly's always in the room. And Max continues to be weird about us at school, claiming I'll lose friends if we're spotted together.

I never know what she'll wear or what kind of mood she'll be in. I prefer the confident side of her that puts me in my place and isn't interested in girl stuff like dresses and makeup. I also like it when she wears her hair loose around her face. Then I have an excuse to tease her about it and brush it behind her ear. It's the closest I've been to touching her in any way that challenges the unspoken boundaries she's set between us.

She doesn't talk much about herself. She once mentioned she moved in with her grandma because she didn't get along with her mom. When I asked about her dad, she only said he wasn't around.

During Christmas break, she stops by every single day. A few of those days, she spends the entire time in Shelly's room, and I only see her when they come out for food. Then, a few days after Christmas, my mom takes Shelly shopping in Mankato, and I'm finally given a chance to be alone with Max. Shelly and my mom invited Max to join them, but lucky for me, Max declined. I wish I knew if it was because she wanted time with me or didn't want to shop.

When she first arrives, she curls up on the bench in our kitchen nook, nibbling on one of my mom's homemade cinnamon rolls with one knee under her chin. Her red and black flannel, black Nirvana T-shirt, and black jeans remind me of my goal to buy her a ticket to a concert for her birthday. It's easy to imagine her enjoying a mosh pit.

"What do you want to do today?" I ask. "We could go skating on the lake or catch a movie in Marshall."

With a shake of her head, her lips tighten. "Let's just hang out here."

"We always hang out here."

"Exactly. Why fix something that isn't broken?" She pops the rest of the roll into her mouth and slides out from the bench. "Why would we want to go to the movie theatre when there are hundreds of your mom's tapes we still haven't watched?"

I suppose she's right. The whole point of going to a theatre would be so we could sit close in the dark, away from my family. Now that they're not home…

She stops in front of the refrigerator to study a picture of my mom in uniform next to a little girl she had once saved. "Does your mom like being a nurse?"

"She says it can be stressful working in the ER, but she likes helping people," I tell her. "The girl in that picture would've died if my mom hadn't realized she was drowning a second time after she had been rescued from drowning in the lake."

"I would like helping people," she says quietly.

I nod, agreeing it would be fitting. She's always helping my mom and Shelly when she's here and doesn't ask for anything in return. "Like my mom says, most nurses have a generous heart. I bet you'd be good at it."

"I don't know…college is really expensive."

"With your grades, you'd easily qualify for scholarships."

She spins around to face me. "What do *you* want to do after high school?"

"I'm not sure exactly what, but something with computers," I admit. "My science teacher got me into robotics. Whatever I end up doing, I hope one day I can afford to live in a city like New York."

"You're such a nerd," she teases, pursing her lips.

One of these times, I won't be able to stop myself from touching those tulip-like lips to finally find out if they're as soft as they appear.

"We could do a marathon of slasher flicks," I suggest, thinking it would be cool if she got freaked out and snuggled up against me. "My mom bought the final Jason movie."

She gives a little involuntary shiver. "I don't like being scared."

There goes that idea. "What about *Jurassic Park*? That one looks cool."

"Isn't that the one where they make an amusement park with dinosaurs? Sounds like a bad idea to me." Her little nose scrunches. "Let's pick something out together."

When she starts for the door leading into our entertainment room in the basement, I catch her forearm and run my thumb along the soft skin on her wrist. "Max, wait."

She turns to watch my thumb repeatedly sweep over her wrist for a moment before she glances up, holding my gaze.

Excitement hits me like a thunderbolt.

I want this.

I want her.

"What do you *want*, Noah?" she impatiently snaps as if she can read my mind.

As she yanks free from my grip, I take a step back, reeling from the angry reaction. For a second, I thought she was into what I was offering. Now I'm not so sure.

"Sorry, I just…" Catching a dark look of warning reflected in her eyes, I wipe the damp palms of my hands against my jeans. "Never mind."

———

On New Year's Eve, my mom has me invite Max to the annual neighborhood party. She hasn't been back since the day we were alone in my basement, watching half a dozen Disney movies from our childhood. Weirdly enough, I don't think she had seen a single one until that day. She became quiet after I touched her arm and clung to the opposite side of the couch. So I was surprised when I called about the party, and she said she would come over if she could bring her little cousin.

Turns out Max's "little" cousin isn't as young as I expected. She's a gangly kid with long blond hair and big blue eyes. When she first steps into my entertainment room alongside Max, I swear the intensity of her eyes makes it hard to breathe.

Both girls wear dresses with floral prints, but the little cousin's is much shorter and fits tight against her thin body. She's clearly way too young for me to even look at, but it's hard not to acknowledge she's on her way to becoming a knockout.

"Noah, this is my cousin, Britta," Max tells me. "She's staying at our grandma's while her mom is in Hawaii."

"It's so lame she wouldn't take me with her," Britta says with a cute roll of those big blue eyes. "But I stole some of her weed, so we're even." She digs in her little white purse and pulls out a joint. "Want some?"

I blink several times, shocked that a pubescent girl is offering me weed. Even Max doesn't act weirded out by the idea. I've smoked it a few times, but usually with guys my age. What kind of people raised Max and her cousin?

"Maybe later," I say once I've recovered. I point up at the ceiling. "We better wait until those guys are so bombed they won't care if they smell it."

"Whatever," Britta replies, shrugging before plopping onto the sectional couch. "So, what are we watching?"

"Your cousin and I will pick something," I volunteer, guiding Max over to where my mom's movie collection is stored inside a closet custom-built by my dad. "How old is she?" I whisper to Max.

She snorts while scanning a shelf of the most recent titles. "Eleven going on twenty."

I touch her arm, waiting for her to turn to me before I ask, "Are we okay?"

"Of course." A bright smile parts her lips. "Why wouldn't we be?"

"You haven't stopped by in a couple of days. I worried you were mad about…something."

Her eyes dramatically roll to the ceiling. "I was busy entertaining Brit."

I don't push the subject further, not wanting to spoil the mood.

We decide on the first *Vacation* movie and settle down next to each other on the couch. An hour in, Max falls asleep, resting her head on my shoulder. It's tempting to wrap an arm around her and pull her close. But I'm worried she'll wake up and think I'm a total creep.

"Are you two doing it?" Britta asks, her voice a little louder than a whisper.

"What?" I snap my head in her direction. "Why would you ask that?"

"It's kinda obvious the way you two flirt."

"We're just friends," I say, leaving out how much I want more.

"Whatever." She rips into one of the candy boxes my mom keeps on the coffee table as part of a "movie night" display. After popping a piece of mint chocolate into her mouth, she asks, "Has she told you why she's living with our grandma?"

I take a minute to think about it. Should I answer honestly or lie? As much as I want to learn the truth, talking about Max when she's asleep doesn't feel right. What if she's only pretending? "She said she doesn't get along with her mom."

"At least she's not lying to you. But that's only a small part of the truth. You're probably not ready to deal with the reality of her situation." After eating the single piece of candy, she tosses the mostly full box back onto the table. "You got anything good to drink around here? Beer? Wine? Whiskey?"

"I'm not getting an eleven-year-old drunk," I mutter, carefully running a jittery hand through my hair without disturbing Max. I glance down at my sleeping friend, scolding myself for being a coward. I should've asked her to be my girlfriend weeks ago.

Most importantly, I shouldn't be talking to her devious little cousin behind her back. For all I know, this girl is a habitual liar.

"So what's the rest of the story?"

Britta's eyes shine with mischief. "It'll cost you."

"I don't have much for cash," I say, shaking my head. *This is wrong.* "I won't have a job until the pool opens next summer."

"Cool beans, you're a lifeguard, but I wasn't talking about money."

Pangs of unease twist through my stomach. "What the hell are you talking about then?"

"There has to be *some kind* of booze you can swipe from upstairs without anyone noticing."

"I'm *not* getting an eleven-year-old drunk," I repeat, trying to mimic my dad's strictest tone. "Do you know how much trouble I could get into? People go to jail for supplying to minors."

She crosses her arms and sinks back onto the couch with a sigh. "Then I guess you're not gonna hear the rest of your wanna-be girlfriend's story."

At some level, I'm aware giving into this bratty kid's bribe is a bad idea. I should give Max a chance to tell me for herself.

More than anything, however, I want to learn the thing Max is too afraid to tell me.

CHAPTER 8
PRESENT DAY

Maxine

Britta's remembrance of life service is held eight days after her death in a ballroom at Key Largo, the other lakeside restaurant and bar. The building's plethora of windows provides a stunning view of the outdoor tiki bar and a smattering of tables overlooking the lake where the boats of several attendees, including Noah's speedboat, are moored to a maze of docks. The ballroom's hardwood flooring and punched tin ceiling give an elegant vibe even without the lavish bouquets of white flowers and white linen on the tables.

Both locals and some of Britta's business connections who have flown in from all across the country pack the space. Since Taylor insisted on following her mother's wishes to be cremated and Britta's body has yet to be examined by a forensic expert, Britta's family decided to proceed without her ashes.

Oliver hired security and paid extra for a private event inside the ballroom to ensure the news media wouldn't crash the party. Several photographers had followed Taylor's fiancé from the airport, hoping for a shot of Britta's grieving daughter.

When we first arrived, as the staff and Britta's family were setting up for the service, I'd hugged Oliver out of obligation. It felt necessary with Taylor and Britta's family as witnesses. The embrace was rather stiff and unnatural on both ends. As far as I'm concerned, I won't have anything to do with him again until Taylor's wedding.

I only spent a few minutes paying respects to my cousin. One of her professional headshots sat on an easel, surrounded by an obnoxiously grand spray of white roses. Her bright smile, sparkling blue eyes, and perfect hair in the photograph made me uneasy in a way I couldn't explain.

For the remainder of the service, I camp out on a stool alongside Taylor and Gabby at the boat-shaped bar on the restaurant side of the building. Taylor wanted nothing to do with the throng of mourners, and I can't say I blame her.

Amidst the twang of country music, we're outnumbered by patrons wearing swimsuits and sporting burns from playing in the sunshine. Christa, a pretty bartender with striking eyes and an appropriate amount of sass, ensures our drinks are always full.

Lingering outside the French doors leading into the ballroom, Oliver portrays the part of a grieving husband with surprising ease. Beyond him, Noah socializes with mourning guests like a candidate at a rally, working his way around the ballroom to visit with old friends and Britta's extended family.

My gaze flutters across the packed bar, settling on Detective Kelly camped out in a quiet corner. She occasionally either sips soda from a straw or glances down at the menu in front of her like a regular patron. Several times, I've caught her observing the room of mourners through the glass windows separating the bar from the ballroom.

As often as she studies Oliver, I wonder if he's an official suspect. Has she followed up on my suggestion to check the flight logs for his shared airplane?

"Mom would've hated all these white roses," Taylor muses between sips of her tap beer. "I tried to tell Aunt Ronda, but she insisted anything else would've been tacky."

"It's still a step up from those dreadful carnations your father suggested," Gabby reminds her, tapping her blood-red manicured fingernails against her glass. "I mean, the *nerve* of that man. He could afford to fly Martha Stewart in to decorate this place with angel wings and fairy dust, but he'd do anything to save a buck. If I'd been in the room when he suggested carnations, he would've had a stiletto permanently wedged up his ass."

"Angel wings and fairy dust?" I ask with a snort. "Really?"

Gabby waves frustrated hands through the air. "You know what I mean. Our Brit deserved the very best."

Taylor giggles for a moment, then catches the condensation on her glass with a finger, all at once somber. "Do you guys think he killed her?"

Gabby throws me a wide-eyed look. "The police are still looking into it, sweetie," she offers, patting Taylor's forearm. "But if he *was* involved, you can bet your pretty little butt—"

Taylor's great aunt, Ronda, approaches with a crass look. She's a stout woman with a neck like a bulldog's and curly hair dyed as black at night. Although I'm not related to the woman since she's a sister of Britta's father, I've spent more time around Ronda than I'd prefer. She was in attendance for each of Britta's life events and repeatedly makes a point to show her disdain for my existence.

Still, I'd rather deal with her than Britta's mother. With the decline of my aunt's memory, it was decided she would be better off left at the memory care unit. Last Taylor had heard, her grandmother refused to believe she was old enough to have an adult daughter.

"You need to come back in and converse with your mother's friends," Ronda scolds Taylor. "They're here to seek comfort from others who loved her. Your poor fiancé has been stuck talking to a strange couple from New York for over an hour. Now's not a good time to become intoxicated." While anxiously fingering the cross hanging from a dainty gold chain around her neck, she shoots me another disapproving look.

I return a wide-eyed stare, wishing I dared to say all the sharp things burning against my tongue. "Did you need something, Ronda?"

"I like your necklace, *Ronda*," Gabby interrupts. "My husband was wearing something almost identical when he died in a fiery car crash. The paramedics said it was melted into his chest."

Mumbling something under her breath, Ronda finally scampers away.

"Good one," Taylor tells Gabby, giggling. "Guess I better go *save* Payton. God knows how much up-and-coming producers hate socializing." She slugs down the rest of her beer before trailing after her pretentious aunt.

"She'll be okay, right?" I ask Gabby.

"Are you kidding me? That kid was born to dominate the world. She's got her mother's stubborn independence and balls-to-the-wall determination."

A set of strong arms encircle me from behind. A heartbeat later, my husband's designer fragrance of citrus and nutmeg fills my next breath.

"How're you holdin' up, sweetheart?" he whispers, his beard hairs tickling my ear.

I sink into his embrace. As much as I resisted being reunited with him initially, he's become my rock. I may not have survived the last week without him.

"Would it be considered rude to leave early?" I whisper back, folding my arms over his.

"Not at all." He presses a lingering kiss against my temple, then brushes his nose across my cheekbone. "You've been through a lot."

His cell phone chimes with an incoming text. I've

learned to accept that it's constantly chirping or ringing at the highest volume possible. Even though he's always making business deals and doesn't want to miss anything involving his corporation, it's annoying.

I spin around as he retrieves his smartphone from the pocket of his pants to check the screen. A chill ripples through my core as his gaze clouds over with irritation, and his mouth pulls into a tight line. I could count on one hand how many times I've seen him angry since the first day we met.

"What is it?" I ask, touching his wrist. "What's wrong?"

"Nothing for you to worry about." He shoves his phone back into his pocket. His comforting smile returns before he drops a kiss inside my hair. "Work stuff."

"Get her outta here, handsome," Gabby tells him. She glances over her shoulder to eye Oliver with blunt displeasure. "I think the *grieving* widower might be gearing up to give a bullshit eulogy or whatever it takes to shift the focus and make this about him. I'm heading out after this drink. We've all endured enough ridiculousness for one day."

By the time Noah and I say our obligatory good-byes to Taylor and Britta's family, the sun has begun to set over the tranquil lake. The deep red hue blends with the glowing lights stretching along the restaurant's small lighthouse, creating a picturesque backdrop.

When Noah holds my hand as we cross through the grassy backyard to descend the wooden stairway leading to the docks, he's still visibly tense.

He's clearly unsettled by whatever he'd seen on his phone.

Uncomfortable silence lingers in the warm summer air on the short boat cruise back to our house. Setting my clutch down, I head over to the sleek bar in the kitchen corner to pop the cork on a chilled bottle of Prosecco. While pouring the sparkling wine into a stemless champagne flute, Noah settles in close behind, gripping my hips.

"What was so upsetting in that text?" I demand, regretting that I hadn't waited to ask when I could witness his expression.

"There was a mix-up in the agreement I made with our new clients from Tokyo. It's not something you need to worry about, I swear. It'll be sorted out soon enough."

The apparent lie spews so smoothly from his lips that I wonder how long he's been dishonest about other things. I take a long swig of Prosecco, feeling only somewhat comforted by the bubbles slipping down my throat and warming my belly.

His warm fingers sweep my wavy hair away from my neck. "Talk to me, sweetheart. I know you're hurting without Britta. Tell me what I can do to help you get through this."

I release an exasperated sigh. "She's *gone*, Noah. There's nothing you can say or do to bring her back."

"Of course not, but I hate seeing you in so much pain." His soft lips and smooth beard hairs dust across my jaw. "Would it help if we went somewhere, just the two of us? We could go back to St. Thomas. You loved it there. It'd take your mind off things for a while. We could stay until they've arrested her killer."

Setting the glass down, I spin to face him with a chill braiding around my spine. "What makes you so sure the killer will be caught?"

"You're not in Chicago anymore. This is a small community. You remember what it was like around here." He swipes a bottle of imported beer from the beverage refrigerator and pops off the top, shrugging. "Unless some random traveler with violent tendencies was passing through, which I highly doubt is what happened, the person who did this will eventually screw up and expose themselves. Small towns, small minds."

Scoffing, I rub my hands over my bare arms. "I didn't realize you were an expert on murder."

"My ex was into true crime, made me watch a lot of documentaries on this kind of thing." He takes a chug of the beer before continuing. "Stabbing usually implies the murder was intimate—the killer had a personal connection with the victim."

Laughter clings to my throat. "Maybe you should be working alongside that detective."

With a shrug, he slowly shakes his head. "I'm just telling you what I learned."

"Which *ex* was this? You hardly ever talk about either of them." Come to think of it, I know little about his second wife beyond her name and pictures I've seen of her on social media. Neither of his wives appeared to have aged well, with unnaturally stiff faces pumped full of collagen.

"You said you didn't want me to talk about them." He says this with a harmless chuckle before he realizes I'm still agitated. Confusion shines in his gaze. "When we reconnected, you told me you wanted to leave everything that happened in the past behind us. You made a point of saying the people we were before we met are now *irrelevant*. I assumed that meant you didn't want to discuss my first marriages."

A dark shadow passes over me as I dwell on the

truth. *The man I married is essentially a stranger. The sixteen-year-old who wanted to protect me is long gone.* "What went on in your second marriage? Was she the problem, or was it something you did? And what about other past relationships? I've heard the rumors about you since I moved here. Who else have you slept with?"

He holds his hands out at his sides. "Sometimes figuring out how to please you is like trying to decipher hieroglyphs. Are you being serious? Why are you asking me that *now*?"

Before I can answer, my cell phone buzzes from my clutch. I retrieve it to find Taylor's face on the screen. Shuffling away from Noah, I answer the call.

"Max?" Taylor cries. "Can you please come get me?"

"Sweetie, what's wrong?"

"It's Dad...he told me—" her voice breaks and she pauses, letting out a stifled cry. She sniffles, then says, "I can't talk about it right now. Will you just come here?"

"Of course. I'm on my way." I grab my clutch and double-check my key fob is inside. "I'm taking the car, so it'll be a good fifteen minutes."

"Just please hurry." Her voice wavers on the verge of more tears. "I'll be waiting outside behind

Pelican Cove. I can't deal with anyone else right now."

"Hang tight, kiddo. It'll be okay."

Noah strokes his beard with one hand as I end the call. "Everything alright?"

"Taylor's dad said something to upset her."

Red blotches fill his cheeks. "Do you think that asshole—"

I hold up a hand to stop him from saying anything more. "I don't have time for this right now. I'm taking Taylor to her mom's. I have a feeling I won't be back tonight." I take a moment to study his defensive pose. "A bit of distance might be what we need right now anyway."

As I spin away from him, he calls out, "Come on, sweetheart. Let's talk. Don't leave things like this!"

A disturbing reality settles in my bones once I'm backing my Mercedes out from the 3-stall garage.

Detective Kelly never mentioned the method by which Britta was killed. I assumed she'd been either knocked out or held underwater before she drowned.

Why does Noah think she was stabbed?

CHAPTER 9
24 MONTHS EARLIER

Maxine

The Friday evening after reuniting with Noah on the beach, I head down to Britta's dock right as he's crossing the still bay. My knowledge of speed boats might fill a thimble, but I'm well aware his must be considered luxurious based on those we've seen around the lake all week. Its dark color and sleek shape suit Noah's exceptional looks. Twin engines purr when he races past a flock of birds, shooting a delightful thrill into my bones.

I was initially worried he'd become an arrogant

Playboy of sorts. But that opinion quickly changed after Britta and I spent the last several evenings with him at Pelican Cove, the lakeside bar on the north end of their bay. He wasn't as flirtatious or boisterous, and he made me laugh countless times until tears rolled down my cheeks. It was like the past 30 years had never happened.

After landing the boat parallel to the dock, he takes my empty hand as I step barefoot onto the deep aft deck with my sandals in my other hand. Britta had insisted I wear one of her low-cut sundresses with a high slit exposing one leg. By the way Noah's intent gaze takes in my curled hair before dusting over the dress, he must appreciate my decision to take her advice.

He makes a pair of tan khakis and a black, fitted polo shirt even more tantalizing than the swim trunks he'd worn the other day. It's difficult to swallow when I recall the sight of his firm stomach and tanned, muscular chest.

My knees weaken when his warm lips brush over my cheek and I'm surrounded by a cloud of his rich cologne. "You look…wow." He backs away, grinning. "Are you hungry?"

"Starved," I admit with a nervous smile.

I perch on the passenger's seat, and we return to

his side of the lake in a blink of an eye. Once the boat is secured to his dock, he gives me a brief tour of his house while the chef prepares our dinner.

With every detail Noah explains, it occurs to me that he's even more wealthy than Britta had insinuated. I'm so pleased to witness his success that my cheeks soon hurt from grinning.

The stone countertops were brought in from Rome. The master bathtub, with a hundred individual jets, from Paris. The rustic beams were reclaimed from an old barn. The rafters had to be reinforced to support the weight of the colossal fireplace stones laid from floor to ceiling. Almost everything was custom-made.

I don't sense he's trying to impress me. I believe he's genuinely proud of his beautiful home, as he should be.

Once we begin a candlelit dinner on one of many paved levels of patios in his backyard, I remember all the reasons I adored him as a teenager. As we dine on edamame and cabbage soup before we're served sushi prepared several different ways, he's attentive to my every need. He doesn't ask about my past. Instead, he provides updates on his family and tells me the details of the company that made him wealthy.

After dinner, we head to the north side of the lake

in his boat. I take my time in admiring him when he's focused on steering around the other boats out for a night cruise. There's something about a firm jaw with a perpetual "day-old" stubble that I find maddeningly attractive, especially on a man Noah's age. If nothing sexual happens and I never see him again, I'll be able to rely on the memory of him perched on the captain's seat in a modelesque pose to keep me warm at night.

We return to the center of his bay as the sun's setting. The lake's glass-like surface reflects the sky's pinkish gold hue tinged with streaks of purple. His stately house in the distance glows from landscaping lights all around the property, its colossal bay windows and peaked roof appearing fortress-like.

Noah kills the engines. We slowly drift along, enjoying the peaceful night with Joe Bonamassa's smooth voice and the chirp of frogs as our soundtrack.

Tears spring to my eyes when I'm all at once reminded of the magical night we shared as teenagers under the same sky.

Something extra special had developed between us. And I ruined it.

"Are you alright?" Noah asks, his voice gentle. He leans in close enough to touch.

Using the back of my hand, I swipe the moisture

from my eyes. "Thanks for this evening," I tell him, attempting a smile. "That sushi, the boat ride, this sunset…it's all truly spectacular. I'm glad I agreed to come out with you."

"I've been meaning to apologize for the day we ran into each other at the beach. I'm sorry if I came on kind of strong." He ducks his chin in a bashful gesture. "Sometimes I feel the urge to exert my masculinity around Britta."

"She can be intimidating."

"I've missed you," he blurts, his expression all at once heavy with regret. "I missed *us*. Every day since you left. I wondered where you went, what you were doing with your life." His eyes glisten in the moonlight. "I was so worried about you, Max."

Wild beats of my heart rattle my entire body. How do I respond? Simply because I missed him just as much doesn't mean we should've kept in touch. It doesn't mean we should've stayed together.

His fingertips brush over my cheek. "You seem happy….maybe even healed. Are you?"

I press my lips together. How does he expect me to answer? Does he want me to lie and say the nightmares have gone away? Does he want me to pretend that after I left him, I lived out a happily ever after?

"Let's not ruin a nice evening," I say, pulling his

hand away from my face. "Everything that happened in the past should stay there, Noah." At a loss for any more words, I sip from the tumbler of wine he'd poured before we left the house. "Britta tells me you've been married a couple of times. Do you have any children?"

Disappointment in my non-answer flashes in his eyes before they wander across the bay. "I wanted children for a few years, but after becoming CEO of Innovative Securities, I realized it wouldn't be fair to them if I was always away on meetings." He's quiet for a minute, reflecting on his choices before his eyes return to me. "What about you? Any exes? Kids?"

"One ex-husband, no children. I met Roger after I graduated from the U of M. He was friends with Oliver."

I don't provide a reason for our breakup or expound on the fact that I stayed on birth control when Roger thought we were actively attempting to conceive. My therapist at the time fully supported my decision. I simply wasn't willing to bring an innocent being into the world. I won't ever be.

"I'm glad you made it to the U," he tells me. "I know how much you wanted to become a nurse." He takes a swig from his tumbler of wine. "I'm glad you agreed to come out with me tonight, Max. I know your cousin more or less steamrolled you into the idea."

"It's nothing personal," I admit, flashing a guilty grimace. "I'm just not much into dating." Life's a lot less complicated without having to hide the details of my complicated life from someone close to me.

"I'm glad Britta backed out. I wanted you all to myself. I know you have a flight out tomorrow, but I'd enjoy another chance to spend time with you— the *adult* you."

Brushing a strand of my hair behind my bare shoulder, his warm fingers linger against my neck. It's something he did a hundred times when we were kids. "In all this time, I haven't met anyone I enjoy being around as much as I enjoyed being with you."

Hundreds of memories from all the times I visited his parents' house come flooding back with his touch. *He told me he loved me.* Violent flutters of anticipation erupt in my belly as I attempt to swallow.

"You're still so unassuming," he explains, "exactly the way I remember you. Most women are all over me, hoping to enjoy the benefits of my wealth. Yeah, it's different because we've known each other since high school, but when I gave you the tour of my house tonight, you seemed...*proud*. I could feel it." With a charming smile, he cups my neck. "And you're so damn beautiful, Max. I'm drawn to the attractive woman you became every bit as much as anything else. I genuinely enjoy every minute we're together."

Until now, I didn't realize my complex feelings for him hadn't wavered.

Once he realized I wasn't like other girls for a long list of unsettling reasons, he was still kind and patient with me.

"What do you want from me, Noah?" I whisper, fighting against a rush of tears. "Like you said, I'm leaving tomorrow."

"Is there a reason you *have to* go back?" he asks.

I shrug half-heartedly. "Work."

Noah shakes his head like he's disappointed in my answer. "The other night, you told me you hate your job. Life's too short to do something that makes you unhappy."

A sharp laugh bubbles from my lips. "Not everyone has the luxury of doing whatever they want, Noah. I have a steep rent to pay…and other bills."

"Have you ever thought of moving out of Chicago and starting somewhere new, maybe take up nursing again?" With a grin that I feel in my toes, he sweeps his thumb over the slit in the dress that reveals my bare thigh. "You'd easily find a decent house around here with the amount you spend on rent in the city. And last I heard, the local clinic needs more nurses."

While I became a registered nurse because I wanted to help people, my role with the hospital has transformed into something different. Still, I choose not to explain how I had actually removed myself from working the hospital floor.

"You're suggesting I uproot my life and relocate to rural Minnesota?" I clarify, my eyes growing wide. "Who does that?"

His grin becomes enduringly crooked. "Why not? Is there someone in Chicago you'd miss? A boyfriend, or—"

"There's no one," I assure him with a quick shake of my head. *I don't even have friends.*

My duties are remote enough that I could possibly continue to perform them while living in another state. At least until something else comes along. Still...

His fingers continue to trace a circle against my skin. "I bet your cousin would let you stay with her until you got on your feet and found your own place."

"What you're suggesting is crazy," I tell him.

"Is it, though?" He slides his hand over mine, linking our fingers together. His touch against my palm sends a sweep of pleasant warmth shooting down to my toes. As he moves in closer, his eyes become hooded. "If you lived here, we'd be able to spend more time together. Like tonight. Or, if you want, we could hang out like we did in the old days, only instead of VCR tapes in a dingy basement, we'd watch movies in my theatre room on the big screen." A boyish grin twists his lips. "But I'm not inviting anyone else to hang with us as a buffer this time."

Swept away by nostalgia, my lungs give a little squeeze. "That does sound tempting."

Now mere inches away, his tongue wets his lips. "Would it be alright if I kissed you?" he whispers. "I miss the taste of that beautiful mouth."

"We barely know each other," I wheeze, woozy with desire. "We're different people."

"No, we aren't," he insists with the start of a sad smile. "Deep down, we're the same sixteen and seventeen-year-olds who cared deeply for each other."

I want to believe him and trust that he's right. But I'm afraid of what will happen if I let myself fall for him a second time. Still, something about his heated gaze convinces me to give in. *He still loves me.*

"Okay," I rasp.

He leans in to brush my lips with his, cautiously caressing them as if asking another question.

Shivers spread down my spine.

It's not due to the sudden and overwhelming desire for this handsome man—my old friend.

We're being watched.

———

The next day, I return to Chicago as planned.

I only stay long enough to get my affairs in order.

CHAPTER 10
21 MONTHS EARLIER

Maxine

Noah's lake-side home, soon to be mine as well, is already bustling with caterers, decorators, florists, and photographers when the doorbell chimes.

Although everyone had arrived before the sun, I was already awake, unable to sleep without Noah at my side. He'd reserved the basement of the neighbor's rental home for himself and his groomsmen, wanting to follow the tradition of not seeing his bride until the ceremony.

Sometimes I want to pinch myself. How did someone like me manage to reconnect with an old flame who has become both ridiculously romantic and exceptionally handsome? I don't deserve him.

I was relieved when he expressed a desire for an intimate ceremony on his lawn with only our closest friends. I didn't want an elaborate white dress in a church where I'd be forced to confess "my love" in front of hundreds of strangers the first time. Roger's Catholic mother had insisted on it.

Roger's family was shocked when I didn't invite anyone other than Britta and Oliver. I can only imagine my ex-in-laws' dismay when they realized how much money they'd blown on a wedding destined to fail from the beginning.

Since Noah's mother passed from a stroke several years back and his feeble father didn't think he could make the trip from his retirement condominium in Fort Myers, his sister, Shelly, is his only family member in attendance.

I was admittedly nervous about reuniting with her until Noah explained she'd become an acclaimed stylist in Los Angeles and wanted to do the bridal party's hair and makeup.

When the doorbell chimes again, I let out an exasperated sigh. "Why isn't anyone answering the door?" I ask.

Behind me, Shelly teases my brown curls with a comb. Although Noah had requested I wear my hair down to flow over my bare shoulders, she insists on a complicated up-do that wouldn't go flat from the lake's infamous gusts of wind.

"Let someone else get it," Shelly tells me. "I need at least another twenty minutes with you."

"I'll get it!" Gabby offers, setting her empty flute of champagne next to the mess of styling products littering the vanity.

I giggle as my friend scurries barefoot from the master bathroom, rollers bouncing in her bleached blond hair, the satin pink robe I'd gifted each of my bridesmaids gaping open. The deep valley between her massive breasts and a hint of her round, "menopausal belly," as she calls it, are fully on display when she slips out of sight.

I adore how she projects herself with the same confidence and ease as Britta. In the short time since we met, I've learned to embrace my less-than-perfect body and its flaws. It also helps that my future husband worships my body like I'm the most beautiful woman in existence.

I'll admit, Gabby was added as a bridesmaid only because Noah told me I had to have three brides-maids to offset the three buddies he'd hand-selected to stand up with him. Since I have yet to make other friends in the area, Gabby was my only choice. Still, I'm convinced it's not something I'll regret anytime soon.

"She's a riot," Shelly comments.

"You ain't seen nothin' yet," Britta tells her with a snigger. "Wait until she gets drunk later. She'll be a total shit-show on heels." Britta rises from the director's style chair at my side and snags the champagne bottle from the stand filled with ice, topping off all 3 flutes of champagne. "I still can't *believe* you're getting married again, Max. I was convinced you'd die alone, surrounded by a horde of annoying cats who wouldn't think twice about eating their master."

"That's a mean thing to say to your cousin," Shelly comments while twisting a lock of my hair behind my ear and pinning it in place. "Max, our mom would've been so pleased to see you and Noah finally end up together. I realize I don't know you like before, but you're a total knockout. My brother is one lucky man."

With such high praise from someone like her, my cheeks burn hot. Shelly is at least six feet tall with bright green eyes that appear cartoonish with liner and eyeshadow. Her hair's shaved short on one side, bleached colorless on the other.

I worry my sleeveless, open-back wedding dress won't hold a candle to her fashionable off-white tunic with wide-legged pants. "You were always too kind to me," I say.

"You're right, you don't know her anymore," Britta snaps, eyes rolling to the ceiling. "She would've died happy with those flesh-eating cats."

Truthfully, I was equally as surprised when I accepted Noah's proposal only a month into our second courtship. The moment he got down on one knee and asked feels like something out of a dream —all muffled voices and fuzzy edges. It's almost as if I was someone else, watching it happen from above.

Britta snags her phone from the disarray covering the vanity and starts for the door. "I'm going to try calling Taylor again. I can't believe that little brat is too hungover to get her hair done in time for her own godmother's wedding."

"You're the one who insisted everyone take shots last night," I remind her before she's gone from sight.

As I sip my champagne, Shelly's green gaze meets mine in the mirror. "No offense, but your cousin seems nicer on social media."

"She has her moments," I say with a slight shrug. "She's probably the most hungover of anyone. She's just a pro at hiding it." I'm sure there's far more to Britta's sour mood, but I won't confide in my new sister-in-law.

Gabby pops back into the room, panting. "Uh, Max, sweetie, your mom is here." She holds a hand next to her mouth and adds in a stage whisper, "I think she's a wee bit drunk."

A hollow spot in the pit of my stomach churns. I hadn't told my mother about the engagement, hoping to avoid the exact scenario I'm now facing.

Since Britta had boasted on social media about her cousin getting married in the same neighborhood in which they'd spent their summers together, I'm sure it wasn't hard for a busybody like my mother to piece together the remaining details. I once considered changing my name so she couldn't find me, but with Britta's involvement, it wouldn't have mattered.

"I'll be back," I announce, removing the cape around my neck and grabbing my phone. I motion for Gabby to take my chair before turning to Shelly. "You better move onto her. This could take a while."

Eyes bright with excitement, Gabby plops into the chair with a smile splitting her face. "Make me look like a fifties movie star, Shelly," she pleads, her voice extra breathy. "Like Marilyn Monroe or Elizabeth Taylor. Not one of those prudish ones, like Aubrey Hepburn or Grace Kelly."

"I'll see what I can do," Shelly tells her as I dart away.

With a growing rush of annoyance, I navigate through the great room. Never-ending boxes of pristine gardenias and white lilies fill the space.

When Noah insisted on taking care of the details, I never imagined he'd go this overboard. Nothing about the grand arbor and white chairs adorned with white satin ribbons, or strings of enormous flower arrangements throughout the backyard could be described as the setting for the "intimate gathering" we'd agreed upon.

Once I discover my mother hanging on the arm of one of the young caterers in the kitchen, her words almost too slurred to comprehend, I'm exceedingly grateful that Noah isn't around to witness my next-of-kin falling apart. Even though Britta once filled him in on the ugly details of our strained relationship, he's unaware of every sordid detail.

"You're making a scene," I hiss sharply, yanking her away from the irritated man. "Sorry," I call over my shoulder before dragging her into the quiet mudroom.

"Don't tell me yer in one of yer *moods*," my mother slurs, lifting a champagne flute to her lips.

I wince. I've worked hard on shedding the accent I picked up while living down south, and I can only hope I never sounded as uneducated.

When our gazes meet, it's like witnessing an older, demented version of myself in 3-decades. We have the same shade of brown hair, although hers comes from a bottle these days and is hacked off at her chin. Our eyes are the exact same blend of hazel and gold. She also has a sharp chin and large ears that, by some gracious miracle, I didn't inherit.

Although she's dressed somewhat appropriately for a lake-side wedding in a dusty-rose dress, the chiffon material is worn, and the floral print has faded. Considering her waning finances, there's a solid chance she picked it up at a second-hand store.

I seize the flute from her questionable grip before she drops it and creates another scene. "You can't attend my wedding in this state."

"Afraid yer husband-to-be will learn the truth from me, are ya? Does he know yer a coward, or is he just taking advantage because yer naive?" Her shrewd eyes drink in every last detail of the room containing high-end, custom cabinets and benches for storage. Dollar signs fill her eyes with every passing moment. "This place sure is fancy. Is this where yer gonna live?"

Tucking a wayward curl behind my ear, I bite my bottom lip. I need her gone, especially before Britta learns she's here and all hell breaks loose. "What will it take to make you relinquish your *right* to be here?"

Her eyes narrow. "Fur today, or fur good? It wasn't cheap to fly here."

"For today, to start." I don't have the time or

energy to deal with her before I'm expected to play the part of a blushing bride.

"Ten grand," she blurts.

I cackle at the ridiculous suggestion. Although I received a decent settlement from Roger in the divorce, my savings are dwindling. It's too soon to borrow a sizable chunk of money from Noah without explaining the situation. "I don't have that kind of cash available."

"Ya sure?" She snags my left hand and scrutinizes my engagement ring. Noah hand-picked the 3-carat emerald cut diamond on a band embedded with another carat's worth of smaller diamonds. It's too flashy for my taste, but he insisted I keep it.

"I can't sell my wedding ring without telling my new husband the truth about you," I snarl, reclaiming my hand and rubbing my fingers like they were doused in fire. "Good luck explaining a valid reason why he shouldn't have you thrown in jail like I should've decades ago."

Expression hard, she sniffs. "Wasn't my fault."

"The judge that sent me to live with Grandma disagreed. It was your job to protect me."

Her gaze snaps over to the far side of the room, too stubborn and possibly too stupid to admit she was wrong.

Still vigorously rubbing my fingers, I shake my

head. "I don't care what it takes to get you out of here, Judy. I need you gone A-SAP. I can get you *five* grand, but it will take time to liquidate the cash. I'll have a private car take you to Sioux Falls. You can stay in a nice hotel until your flight back to Georgia. On me."

Her lips wiggle around as she contemplates the offer. Finally, she concedes, "I s'pose that'll do."

Instead of explaining how messed up a mother must be to bribe her daughter when she's the one in the wrong, I escort her outside and make the arrangements.

———

By the time I return to the master bathroom, Gabby's elegant updo is finished. "Everything alright?" she asks, throwing me a concerned glance almost identical to Shelly's.

Anger from the incident with my unwanted visitor begins to simmer. "Please don't tell Noah about my mother stopping by," I beg them. "I sent her to Sioux Falls before she could make a scene. She's not well and refuses to go to the treatment I've offered countless times. I'd die of embarrassment if Noah learned the truth."

I figure it'll be easier to claim my mother's an

alcoholic in need of help rather than explaining to Noah why I pay her to stay away.

"Honey, your secret's safe with me." Gabby mimes zipping her lips and throwing away the key. "I'm sorry to hear about your mother, but we all have personal demons to fight. There's no reason the rest of the world needs to know they exist."

"Amen to that," Shelly agrees, nodding. "He won't hear a word about it from me."

Moments later, a deep cough fills the room. Noah slides around the corner, one hand held over his eyes. In the white Prada button-down I'd selected to go with his favorite pair of black Gucci slacks and Tom Ford dress shoes, he's worthy of a magazine cover.

"Sorry to interrupt, ladies," he announces. "I just wanted to check on my bride."

"Are you out of your mind?" Gabby squeals, jumping in between us with her arms braced out around her. "You can't see her yet! It's bad juju!"

"That's exactly why I'm covering my eyes," Noah answers amusedly. "Didn't want to stir up any trouble. I just came in to see if there's anything she needs. I want this day to be perfect for her."

"Of course you do," Shelly says with a giggle.

"Damn it, that's sweet," Gabby concedes, dropping her arm. She spins around to face me, her hands cupped over her heart. "I've always dreamed of finding the perfect man," she tells me. "You're the luckiest girl in the world to have found him."

"I know," I tell my friend. With a gracious smile, I move around her and pull Noah into the hallway where I can kiss him in private. When we part, I remove his hand from his eyes. "Thank you for this perfect day," I whisper with a grin playing on my lips.

"Just when I was convinced you couldn't be any more beautiful...you're positively stunning," he utters in a hoarse voice, cupping my face in both hands. His eyes roam over my expertly done makeup and partial hairdo. "I can't wait to spend forever with you, sweetheart. I knew it's what I wanted back when I was seventeen. This day is long overdue."

Tears prick my eyes right as Britta's stern voice breaks the spell between us like a sharp blade. "Then you better let her finish getting ready." She steps in to grab my wrist, yanking me away from my groom. "Honestly, Noah. It's not wise to break tradition. You've done this enough times to know the rules."

Her grip is tight enough to leave red marks on my skin.

CHAPTER 11
PRESENT DAY

Detective Joesphine Kelly

The morning after Britta Baxter's celebration of life service, I grab several cups of black coffee and a homemade breakfast from Trail's Edge, the cozy little corner store down the road from the Huismans' home. The two owners, both retired law enforcement, appreciate when I'm not in the mood for conversation and trying to collect my thoughts, like today. They only stop by when I need my coffee refilled and keep the conversation short.

I've been contemplating following Dr. Baxter back to Minneapolis to monitor his activity for a day or two. It would also give me a chance to stop home. Spending time at the park with Henry would both provide a short break and allow me to collect my thoughts on Britta Baxter's murder.

During the night, I parked across from the home owned by the victim. However, there hadn't been any movement beyond the arrival of Maxine Huisman's Mercedes. I had hoped to catch the neurosurgeon doing something unusual to give me probable cause for an arrest.

Sheriff Jaros calls as I'm chewing on the last bite of my scrumptious biscuits and gravy.

"I'm afraid I'm calling with bad news, Detective," he announces, his voice gruff with irritation and his vehicle's siren wailing above. "We found another body."

My fork clatters down to my plate, causing some of the locals to glance my way. "You're kidding. What's the story with this one?"

"Afraid it's more of the same. Found her floating in Shetek, multiple stab wounds to her back."

I grip the phone a little tighter. "Do we have a positive ID?"

"Don't need one. It's Linda Boese, a bartender from the Legion in Currie."

"You're sure?"

"As sure as I can be. She's been serving me drinks for the last decade."

"How old?"

"I'd say early thirties. One of the gals in my office is collecting Linda's info to send my way. Should receive it any minute."

I briefly close my eyes, silently praying his deputies haven't done anything to disturb the scene's integrity this time. "Where's the body?"

"Still floating in the water as of now. Soon as I'm done talking to you, I'm calling my deputies and the coroner to help retrieve her. You're the first call I made after dispatch relayed the message."

"Who called it in?"

"Donna Rivers, a resident on the east side of the same bay where we found Ms. Baxter. The body came right up to her shoreline. Mrs. Rivers saw the woman's foot, thought it was a bloated carp until she walked down to her dock to get a better look. She screamed loud enough to draw two of her neighbors outside. A third called nine-one-one."

I pull a wad of bills from my pocket, slapping a $20 on the table. I nod my thanks to the friendly owners before heading to the parking lot. "I just happen to be right down the road. I'll be there soon."

Son-of-a-bitch. Guess I won't be getting a break anytime soon.

Several hours after the crime scene is secured, I leave the medical examiner's office to meet with the victim's sister at the sheriff's station in Slayton. My frustration percolates as Molly Boese settles across from me in the same chair where Britta Baxter's husband sat during his interrogation.

I was beginning to believe Dr. Baxter was the perpetrator. In addition to a lack of evidence indicating his involvement in the second murder, however, there doesn't seem to be a connection between the doctor and the newest victim.

Studying the sister, my spine tingles with a feeling my grandma once described as "having someone walk over your grave." Without having to ask, I'm sure Molly and Linda were identical twins. Besides the fact that Linda's mossy green eyes had been lifeless and empty while Molly's swirl with a mix of sorrow and rage, the wheat-blonde sisters shared the exact same button nose and upturned lips on a heart-shaped face worthy of a beauty queen.

Whoever murdered Britta Baxter and Linda Boese had a definite type.

I grab the ballpoint pen left from a previous interview and scribble *"twins"* onto the small notepad I keep in my blazer pocket. I then slide the box of tissues within the sister's reach. "You have my deepest condolences, Miss Boese."

Molly eyes the tissues with misplaced disdain. "I still can't believe it. I just talked to her last night. She sounded so happy."

"What time did your call end?"

"Sometime around midnight. She closed the bar early and was headed to her boyfriend's place."

I nod. The medical examiner had estimated the victim's death to have been relatively recent. "It'd be helpful if you'd check your phone for the exact time."

With a mucus-filled sniffle, the sister lifts her phone from the table and brushes her finger over the screen for a handful of seconds. "It was twelve thirteen."

"Good…that's good." I study the young woman's bloodshot eyes. "What can you tell me about her boyfriend?"

"Not much. I know he lived somewhere on the lake." The woman finally snags a tissue to blot her wet nostrils before crumbling it in her fist. "I think he was married. Linda skated around the subject when I asked her straight up. She claimed it didn't matter, said he was definitely on the market."

"She never mentioned a name or described his looks?"

"Nothing beyond the fact that he was hot and the

best lover she'd ever had." She opens her fist and stares intently as her fingers crush the tissue again. "We haven't been talking as much as usual. We used to spend hours on the phone, telling each other every detail of our lives. It's my fault—I've been busy with work since moving to the cities. I should've called her more...should've made time for visits."

She glances upward, her green eyes heavy with pain. "I don't feel anything. I always thought we shared a physical connection, and I'd feel like I was missing an appendage or something if something like this happened to her. But I feel...numb."

"You're probably still in shock," I suggest in a gentle tone. "The grieving process can take time. It's different for everyone."

The sister's eyes light up. "Did she have her phone on her? She would have his name and number programmed, don't you think?"

"The sheriff's department is looking for it." It's best to spare her the details of how the sheriff is arranging for a diver to search the lake bottom for a murder weapon or anything else that might help with either investigation. "If it doesn't turn up, the court can order the cell phone company to release her records."

"That means if her boyfriend killed her, you can track him down?" Molly asks with a spirited nod.

"It's a possibility. Any idea how long she had been with him?"

"A few months or so. Last week, she told me she thought she might be falling in love."

"Is there anyone in Linda's past who may have wanted to hurt her? Did she have any abusive exes, any patrons at the bar who might have harassed her or made unwanted advances?"

"Not that I know of. Her last boyfriends were all sweet…good ole' local boys with blue-collar jobs. She broke it off with every one of them because they didn't have the income to take care of her the way she wanted. I think that was part of the draw to this new guy—he sounded rich. But like I said, we weren't as close lately as we've been. Back when I lived here, guys flocked to her like flies. She was flirtatious with customers and believed wearing low-cut shirts earned her better tips. I made it clear when I was bartending that I wouldn't tolerate guys getting handsy or suggestive."

"You also bartended at the Legion?"

"No, at Key Largo on the lake. I was only there a couple of summers during college."

The population of permanent residents in the area is reasonably low. If Linda had been dating this man before the official start of summer, he likely lives in the area year-round. If the boyfriend was wealthy, as the sister suspects, I have a few ideas of potential suspects. "Do you have an idea of who this 'hot' married man could be?"

"Maybe. But I haven't lived here in almost a decade. A lot of outsiders have built houses around the lake in that time."

"Linda never sent you any pictures or posted anything on social media of herself with this boyfriend?"

"Not that I can remember. That's part of the reason why I figured he was married. She was way into selfies. It wasn't like her to keep the men she was dating a secret."

"It'd help if you could write down every form of media she used—her user names too, if you know them. A detail in the background of a picture she posted could help identify this boyfriend—something small you might have otherwise missed." I rip a clean sheet of paper from my notebook and hand it to Molly with the pen. "Write down your number, too, in case I have any more questions."

"Whatever you need, Detective," she says as she begins jotting down the information. "I'll be staying with my parents on Keely Island." She glances at me with an expression of determination. "I'm not leaving until the bastard that did this to her is behind bars."

Good, I think. With a pleased smirk, I watch Molly

head to the parking lot and drive away in a red compact car with an "Aussie mom" sticker on the back window. Whether or not the killer knew Linda was a twin, they'll more than likely find it upsetting to see a mirror image of their victim freely walking around town.

CHAPTER 12
PRESENT DAY

Beth

The pull of gratification becomes almost too much to handle as I watch my beautiful lover sleep soundly on his back, one hand tucked beneath his pillow and one leg hooked around the luxurious Egyptian beddin'. He looks so peaceful, like he doesn't have a care in the world.

He's exceptionally handsome, with a faint sliver of moonlight providin' a silhouette of his sculpted jaw, intense nose, and generously curved lips. Although he always sleeps in the nude, the shadows from the trees outside hide his lower half from my hungry eyes. I could stand here until the sun rises, drinkin' him in and revelin' in the fact that I have this beautiful man wrapped around my little finger.

At first, he was reluctant to engage in anythin' beyond vanilla sex. With time, he become ravenous, unable to control the dark urges I extracted from the darkest corners of his desires.

He pretends to portray the image of a good, loyal husband.

Everyone in the community believes it to be true.

Amusement curls my lips. The naiveté of some people never fails to astonish me.

A loose plank of floorin' creaks beneath my weight, and he stirs awake. He shifts around in the king-sized bed, squintin' against the darkness.

"Hey there, darlin'," I whisper in my most seductive of voices, twirlin' a lock of my blond hair. "Did you miss me?"

Rotatin' to his side, he reaches out to turn on the lamp beside the bed. The soft glow highlights his rich brown eyes, glowin' with approval as they skim across the lace details coverin' my naughty bits. "*Beth*?" he calls out, his voice ragged with sleep. "What's this? What are you doing?"

"Were you expectin' someone else, sugar?" I tease.

He scoots into a sittin' position, eyes alight with caution. "No, I just thought…it's been a while. I thought you were…gone."

"That's not the kind of greetin' I was hopin' for. Do you want me to leave?"

Annoyance sharpens his tone when he says, "I'm not in the mood for your games. I took a sleeping pill —you know those make me crazy."

"That's funny because you always seem to thoroughly enjoy yourself when we're playin' games," I reply with a flirty giggle. "Besides, I love it when you're crazy. It brings out your kink."

With a seductive lick of my fire-red lips, I yank on the strings holdin' the skimpy nightie in place. "I thought you might want some company."

His eyes darken as the silky material tumbles down to my belly, exposin' my bare breasts to the cool air.

"Oh hell," he grunts. "How am I supposed to say no to those?" With a resolved groan, he pats the empty side of the bed. "Get in here, beautiful."

Grinnin', I let the nightie fall around my feet before slinkin' down beside him. His lips are ravenous, his hands graspin' for purchase. He's a man starved for pleasure, desperate for passion.

His wife deserves better than this womanizer.

She's naive to think he's ever been a loyal husband.

I'm doin' this to protect her.

In time, I plan to expose the *real* Noah Huisman to the world.

CHAPTER 13
28 YEARS EARLIER

Noah

In the two and a half months since Max somewhat reluctantly agreed to become my girl-friend, I've struggled how to tell her what I learned about her past. Or at least what Britta told me. It might be time to bring my parents into the situation if everything her little cousin said was true.

I'm not sure how to approach the subject. Aside from my dad's stories of working with the dead, I come from a boring family. I was raised by loving parents who would do anything to keep me safe.

At least Max is safe as long as she's in Minnesota.

I haven't seen Britta again since New Year's Eve

when she got stupid drunk on a bottle of my mom's white wine, and Max woke with no idea of what had gone down.

My ass was saved when Max and Britta's grandma called to check in, and my intoxicated aunt told her the girls were sound asleep in our guest bedroom. I almost wish I had answered so I could confirm with Max's grandma all the nasty things Britta had to say about Max's childhood were true.

One night, as we're hanging out on my bed, browsing through the catalog of classes for our upcoming junior year, Max glances up at me while nibbling on her bottom lip. She wears a white T-shirt underneath a green dress that draws out the green in her hazel eyes, and her long brown hair is pulled back with a scrunchie. Taking in every delicate feature on her face and the sweet little flower earrings in her ears, I've never wanted to kiss her so badly.

"What?" I ask. She only chews her lip that way when nervous about something. "What's wrong?"

"I might have to return to my mother's place for the summer," she says. Her eyes all at once shine with tears. "I don't want to go," she adds. 'But—"

"*No*," I bark out. I can't think beyond the surge of red-hot anger rising in my chest. "No way in hell."

Her eyes narrow with suspicion. "Why?"

"Because I'd miss you," I amend, remembering I'm supposed to be clueless about her home life. I soften my tone and attempt to smile. "What would I do by myself?"

A tear slips over her cheek when she glances down. "You're a lifeguard," she mutters. "You'd spend the summer impressing the girls at the pool."

"Not when I have a girlfriend."

When she glances back up, her cheeks flush a dark red. "Still…you'd survive without me around."

She has no idea what this innocent, vulnerable side of her does to me. I'd do anything to keep her from returning to her mother's. I hook my arm around her narrow waist and drag her close, wanting to protect her in any way possible. Her eyes pop wide with surprise.

"You just finally agreed to be my girl," I say, briefly eyeing her lips. I've taken things slower than I'd like only because I get the sense she's not ready for anything beyond holding hands and cuddling. Now that I finally have an idea why she's so emotional, I'm *definitely* not going to push her into anything.

Still, I'm dying to find out once and for all if her lips are as soft as I imagine. "Can't you tell your mom you want to stay here?"

"My grandma's health hasn't been great. They

don't know what's wrong yet, so she has a ton of doctor's appointments scheduled. I think she's worried her insurance won't cover everything. Even though I offered to find a job—"

"You can stay here," I blurt, my mind racing. "You could have the guest bedroom. My parents and Shelly adore you. I'm sure they'd be fine with it."

Her lips part with a quiet gasp. "I can't ask your parents to take me in."

"You don't have to. I'll do it for you."

A little laugh bubbles from her throat, sounding more like a cry. "Noah..." She drops her chin and shakes her head. "It would be better if I wasn't around anyway."

"That's not true." Frustration sparks through my core. How do I express what I'm feeling? How can I explain the raw fear roaring through my veins?

She can't go back to her mom's. I won't let it happen. And I don't know how to tell her without hurting her feelings.

"I think...I mean, I might be..." Heart pounding, I suck in a huge breath. "I'm *in love* with you, Max."

The words hang in the air between us for a moment. Especially when I think she looks *mad* for a minute. More tears slip from her eyes when our eyes lock.

"You can't say that," she whispers. "Don't say that."

"Why not?" I challenge, lightly squeezing my grip around her. "It's the truth."

Her eyes close, and she becomes still.

I feel like a complete asshole, even though I don't understand. How could telling her I love her make her this upset? "Max—"

Her eyelids flip open. "Don't call me that."

I open my mouth to reply, clueless as what to say. If she would rather be called "Maxine," why didn't she tell me months ago?

Watching me with a sexy expression, her tongue wets her lips. She lifts her fingers to dust them back and forth right above the waistband of my jeans. They're shockingly cold against my warm skin.

I jump. She's never done anything beyond holding my hand. I try like hell not to react in any way, but I'm a guy. Some things can't be helped.

"You like that, huh?" she asks, her voice deeper than usual.

Hell yeah, I like it. I *don't* like the way she's acting. I try to swallow, but my throat has become paper-dry. "I think we should talk about the real reason I don't want you to go back to your mom's."

Her lips curl with a teasing smile. "Oh, I know why you want me around." She winks before working on releasing the top button on my jeans. "I'm not stupid."

"Wait." I grab her hand before she can start on the next button. "What are you doing?"

"I know what guys like you want."

"No," I say, my voice firm. "This isn't like you. Can we talk about your mom's boyfriend?"

She yanks her hand from my grip and snarls, "Why would you think that evil witch has *a boyfriend?*"

"On New Year's, when Britta came here with you…she said some things."

"About the boyfriend?" With a brutal laugh, she slides off the bed and folds her arms, barely controlling her anger. "You and Britta had a *private* conversation about somethin' you know *nothin'* about and have no business discussin'? What *else* did you two do together?"

My face turns ice cold. "Nothing. Holy shit, Max. You think I'd do something like that to you? Besides, she's just a kid."

"She's also a big fat liar." She snags her backpack from my desk and slings it over one shoulder. My gut drops with the hateful glare she throws me. "What other secrets are you keepin'?"

"That's it, I swear." I wish I could take back everything I said. I hate seeing her this way. "I was scared to say anything because I didn't want to upset you."

"Well, it's too late for that, isn't it?" she snaps before heading for my bedroom door.

"Max, wait."

She doesn't wait.

———

The following day, my mom's cleaning the kitchen appliances as I'm hunched over a bowl of Oreo O's and milk, trying to wake up. I didn't sleep much after Max stormed out of my bedroom. I was too busy planning a solution to our problem. I won't ask if Max can come live with us unless she agrees to the idea. I also can't let Max put herself in that kind of danger by returning to Georgia.

Maybe my mom can help me figure out what's happening with Max. She's always saying she witnesses a lot of eye-opening mental health things while on the night shift.

"Hey, Mom? Can I ask you something?"

She tosses the cleaning rag over her shoulder and turns to me with one eyebrow raised. The only trait we have in common is our thick, dark hair. She's shorter than average, with pretty green eyes, and a narrow face. My buddies often tell me she's hot, which totally grosses me out.

I have to admit she's pretty compared to a bunch of other moms. More importantly, she's cool and easy to talk to about stuff.

"You need money for the spring dance," she assumes, grinning. "Your dad and I already talked it over. We'll cover the cost of a suit and some nice dress shoes. You probably should have a suit on hand anyway. Whatever flowers and whatnot you want for Maxine needs to come out of your pocket, but we'll loan you whatever you need to cover it until your first paycheck comes."

"Thanks," I say, realizing I haven't asked Max about going. I doubt she would be interested, especially when I doubt she could afford a dress. And it's not like there's anyone she would want to hang out with. I'm pretty sure me and Shelly are her only friends.

My mom's eyebrows shoot upward. "Did you want to ask something else?"

I hesitate to answer right away. I don't want her thinking any less of Max. Besides, I'm not sure what's going on. Maybe she's just upset about the things Britta claims have been done to her, and she doesn't know how to deal with her anger. I wouldn't blame her.

Had she confirmed her mom's boyfriend had molested her, I don't know how I would've stopped myself from driving down to Georgia and kicking that son-of-a-bitch's ass.

"No, that was it," I finally tell my mom while scooping more cereal onto my spoon. "Thanks for being cool about Max hanging around all the time."

"She's a sweet girl. It sounds like she doesn't have an ideal family situation, so I'm glad she gets to spend time with ours."

You don't know the half of it, I think with a silent grunt.

CHAPTER 14
PRESENT DAY

Maxine

Noah snores heavily at my side—a sure sign that the glass of whiskey I spiked with a benzo with his dinner helped him slip into a solid, undisturbed sleep. We haven't had much to say to each other since our fight after the memorial service.

I can't stop thinking about that damn text and wonder what he's hiding. Luckily, he put in a long day locked in his office, only coming out to eat before turning in hours ahead of me.

The half-moon beaming through the wall of bedroom windows makes it effortless to creep around our bed to his side, where his cell phone is plugged into a charger. The sudden urge to wrap the cord around his neck and pull until he stops breathing overwhelms me for a disturbing moment.

I suck in a trembling breath. *I'm no killer*, I tell myself.

Once I've recovered from the ridiculous idea, I remove the charger from the phone's port and lower the screen to his face. When it makes a distinct clicking noise, signaling it's unlocked, I'm struck with a satisfying thrill. I'd been messing around with my phone earlier and was pleased to discover a person's eyes didn't have to be open for the facial recognition to work.

Slipping out of the bedroom on the pads of my bare feet, I silence the phone's ringer before removing all locks in the settings. I head outside to the first patio, settling into one of the couches before beginning my search on Noah's phone. I recognize every contact who has sent him a text in the last twenty-four hours, and I don't find anything that would be considered upsetting.

I browse the dozens of apps, hoping something unusual will catch my eye. I suspect there's an app that would allow him to hide any conversations he wouldn't want his wife to accidentally see.

But after he'd fallen asleep, I'd done some research and learned any recently deleted pictures would still be stored in his phone's folder for up to 30 days. Considering he works in cyber security, it surprising that he's not vigilant with his electronics, and often asks me how to perform certain operations on his phone or laptop. Then again, as CEO of his corporation, he mostly maintains a positive representation of the company and closes multi-million-dollar deals with clients.

Within seconds, I'm staring at the obscene image of a blue-eyed, topless blonde. She's a stunning beauty with flawless skin and spiral curls spilling past her armpits. The symmetrical curves of her abnormally large breasts on her petite frame make me believe she has implants. From the angle of her outstretched arm, it's clearly a selfie. She's standing in front of a bed with a purple comforter and a flatscreen television mounted to a wall behind it.

I wait for tears to sting my eyes or a sense of utter betrayal to punch me in the stomach.

But the logical side of my brain urges me to hold off on any gut reactions. Noah could have an explanation for why this was on his phone. Maybe he was upset because the woman is stalking him, and the picture was unsolicited.

Who are you kidding? a voice ridicules me from a

dark corner of my mind. *He's a womanizer, just like you always suspected.*

As my heart sinks with the thought, I silently scold myself for not making an effort to reach out to either of his ex-wives before agreeing to become his third. My mother was right—I've always been a coward. Most of all, I'm incredibly naive.

———

Martin, my mom's boyfriend, sits beside me, holding my hand. Surrounded by strangers and headstones, the dull voice of a pastor reading from a hymnal saturates the air. Martin's fingernails dig into my skin until blood trickles down, forming a spot on the thigh of my white dress.

"We must repent, Maxine," he tells me. "Repent for our sins."

I turn to discover Noah sitting on my other side. I beg for his help, but I don't think he can hear me because he doesn't react to my cries.

Face soaked with tears, my husband stares at the elegant white ivory casket adorned in blood-red flowers.

Britta's corpse lays inside the casket. Her face is sickly pale as if caked in white makeup, and her lifeless eyes glisten like marbles.

They're fixated on me.

A baby wails in the distance.

With the chime of a doorbell, I gasp for air and bolt upright. My skin and the sheets beneath me are both covered in a sheen of sweat.

It was only a dream.

The doorbell chimes again. I scramble from our bed in search of my robe, relieved to see the suit and dress shoes Noah laid out the night before are gone. He'd mentioned he had a meeting in Bloomington today and would possibly return if everything went as planned. I'm just grateful I don't have to figure out how to confront him about the picture. At least not yet.

Once I've secured my robe around my waist, I glance at the security app on my phone while starting for the front doors. Detective Kelly waits on our front step, impatiently shifting her weight from one foot to another. I haven't seen her since Britta's service. I hoped it meant she was busy arresting someone.

Tight bands of pain grip my chest as I swing open the door. I force past the uncomfortable sensation with a smile.

"Good morning, Detective. Are you here with news on Britta's case?"

"Unfortunately, no." She steps inside, apparently

past the point of niceties. Her expression is grave when she says, "I'm sure you've heard by now about the second body they found floating at the north end of your bay yesterday morning."

A noiseless gasp rips up my throat. "What? No, I —" My pulse quickens as I try to recall the previous day's events. I'd helped Taylor pack some of her mother's sentimental things before she left on a late morning flight. Beyond that, everything comes to me in a jumbled haze.

I'd taken some of the pills Gabby had given me in an attempt to catch up on sleep and calm my paranoia. I'm confident I didn't hear anything about another dead body. "Who was it?"

"Linda Boese, a bartender from the Legion in Currie." The detective retrieves her cell phone from her pants pocket and unlocks the screen.

I come face-to-face with a striking blonde in a cropped T-shirt and short jean shorts at the city's recent street dance on the 3rd of July.

Her smile is both vibrant and all too familiar.

Blood rushes from my head. The house slants.

It's the woman from the topless selfie.

Feeling faint, I reach for the door and squeeze the handle.

A hand grips my elbow. "Are you alright, Mrs.

Huisman?" Detective Kelly asks. "Let's get you over to the couch. I'll grab you a glass of water."

As the detective leads me to the sofa, and my thighs sink into the soft leather cushion, my mind races with gruesome thoughts.

Is that why Noah deleted the woman's picture?

Is he capable of murder?

"Here you go," the detective says, inserting a tepid glass into my hands. "Take slow sips...nice and easy."

When I do as she instructs, it's like I'm watching myself go through the motions from far away. As the room-temperature water trickles down my throat, I try to imagine Noah wielding a knife, thrusting it repeatedly into the woman's naked body.

If he did, in fact, kill her, does it mean he killed Britta too?

No, I insist, firmly shaking my head. *He wouldn't. He knows I loved her.*

"What is it?" Detective Kelly places a hand on my arm. "Did you know the victim?"

"She looks familiar," I manage to choke out, glancing at her fingers on my forearm. I hadn't realized she was sitting beside me until I felt her touch.

She withdraws her hand and offers a kind smile. "I think you went into shock for a minute. From experience, I'd say that reaction indicates you had some kind of relationship with the victim."

"I didn't *know* her," I insist in a firm tone, meeting her questioning gaze with resolve. "I've maybe seen her a time or two around town."

"Mrs. Huisman, has your husband ever been unfaithful?"

There's no way to mask my surprise. My lips fall open before I have a second to reflect on what she's asking. I recover with a scowl. "I don't see how that's any of your business, but no. He's loyal. He would never hurt me that way."

My insides knot with the truth. *That picture…*

She quirks one eyebrow. "Are you certain?"

"What does the sanctity of my marriage have to do with anything?"

"We have reason to believe Miss Boese was having an affair with a married man."

Bile sears my throat. "So the solution is to knock on the door of every married woman in the area and ask if their husband has ever cheated?"

"It's also believed this man was wealthy. Those two factors, in addition to your husband and Britta Baxter having an intimate history—"

"Excuse me?" I slam the glass down onto the coffee table. "I don't know what you think you're—"

"You mean you didn't know?" Amusement lights

the detective's eyes. She's enjoying herself. "Mrs. Baxter and your husband had an affair while he was married to his first wife."

She crosses her arms and leans back against the couch cushions, studying me with a thoughtful expression. "Both your cousin and this woman were stabbed in the back, Mrs. Huisman. That indicates it was a crime of passion. It may also indicate the killer had an intimate relationship with these women and couldn't stand to look them in the eye while hurting them. If you know *anything* about your husband and Miss Boese, now's the time to share those details."

The bile in my throat rises a little higher, leaving an acidic taste.

Noah was right.

Britta was stabbed.

And both Britta and Noah had lied when they first insisted there had never been anything intimate between them.

"Who told you about Noah and Britta?" I demand, my nostrils hardening.

"I spoke with an old classmate of Britta's at the memorial service. She told me Britta was sleeping with Mr. Huisman the summer before her sophomore year of college."

Anger buckles through my core, casting a dark shadow.

Do not sit here and listen to a stranger explain the details of your husband's past like you're some kind of idiot.

"Gossip in these small communities spreads like wildfire, *Detective*," I snap. "Do you have any way of proving those rumors are true?"

The amusement lighting her gaze doesn't diminish with my curtness. "I plan on speaking to your husband to confirm whether it's true, but I've been unable to reach him. When do you expect him back?"

Standing on trembling legs, I fold my arms over my middle. "I think it's time for you to leave."

Detective Kelly rises to her feet and hooks her thumbs inside her belt loops, head tilted to one side. "If you're in any kind of danger...if your husband has been threatening you in any way—"

"Next time you want to speak to either Noah or me, you can arrange an interview through our attorney, Billie Klein, out of St. Paul," I tell her. "I trust you can find her contact information on your own."

Lips tight, she gives a firm nod. "Understood. But you can only ignore the truth for so long."

CHAPTER 15
10 MONTHS EARLIER

Maxine

The morning of our first anniversary, Noah announces we're heading to the airport in four hours and will be spending fifteen days in the Virgin Islands. In a haze of shock and nervous energy, I beg Britta and Gabby to come over and help me pack.

We sip on $100-a-bottle champagne leftover from the wedding while Gabby becomes a cyclone of activity in the walk-in closet. Britta remains quiet at my side in the master bedroom. She places items selected by Gabby inside the Louis Vuitton suitcase

Noah gifted to me before my bachelorette party in Napa Valley.

"I've never been to the Virgin Islands," I say, hoping to pull Britta out of her unusually sullen mood. "Will I need a jacket?"

"A light jacket is never a bad idea when you're going on a tropical vacation," she answers with a shrug. She stops folding long enough to peer up at me. "I've never known Noah to be this spontaneous. You didn't have any idea this trip was coming?"

"You clearly don't know my husband as well as I do," I practically sing, pleased to rub the fact in her face. "He's always planning little day trips and surprising me with things he decides to buy last-minute, like my Mercedes and the new wedding set."

I hold up my left hand, wiggling my ring finger weighed down with several more carats. "He said he couldn't resist buying it when he spotted it in Tiffany's window on his last trip to New York."

Britta's eyes snap back to the contents of my suitcase. "Seems like the kind of thing a man *guilty* of something would do—buy expensive jewelry and plan last-minute trips."

"You're probably right. He's been feeling incredibly guilty that he's always gone on business trips." With a wistful smile, I run my fingers over the silk detail of the sexy designer negligee Gabby gifted me as a shower gift.

"For months now he's been promising to take me somewhere where he can have me all to himself. The man is insatiable." My cheeks warm as the words fall from my lips. The champagne has made me light-headed.

Huffing, Britta unceremoniously tosses a sundress into the suitcase and balls her fists against her hips. "That's not the type of guilt I was insinuating, *Max*. I think maybe he's cheating on you."

"*What*?" Something about her victorious tone sets me off. "Why would you say that?"

"Come on, Max. In all the times he's been away on business, you don't think he's had countless temptations?"

"That doesn't mean he's cheating on me." Lips tight, I shake my head. "You're just jealous that I'm in a healthy marriage."

She lets out a cackle. "That's not what this is. At all."

"You're clearly jealous, Britta, and that's not a good look on you. Are you ready to admit you and Noah had something before I started dating him? Is that what this is about? Are you upset that he asked *me* to marry him instead of *you*?"

Her eyes narrow. "You're delusional."

"Then why would you say such a thing?" I throw my hands up at my sides. "Why are you accusing my husband of something that serious unless you have proof of this so-called infidelity?"

Sucking her lips into her mouth, she glances at the open doorway leading into the living room before her shoulders lower with a great sigh. "Do you know someone named Beth?" She tilts her head and studies me carefully, waiting for my reaction.

Panic swirls through my chest. "Where'd you hear that name?" I demand.

Gabby enters the room with one armful of colorful fabrics and the other glittering with my most valuable jewelry. "Even though you're staying in your own private villa and don't have to impress the staff, it's important you have several different outfits throughout the day to provide your hubby with as much eye candy as possible. I think you're gonna need another suitcase."

She releases an aggressive sigh when she realizes she walked into a tense situation. "What'd I miss? Did someone die?"

"Britta just remembered she has content to create by this afternoon," I say, somehow resisting the urge to give into the sneer tugging at my upper lip. I gesture to Gabby with a friendly smile. "Guess it'll just be me and you packing for this trip."

"Max," Britta pleads, "I'm not saying this to be cruel. I truly believe something is going on with him."

"Who, Noah?" Gabby's eyes widen as she spins around to face Britta. "As in, you think he's sick? Oh, god…do you think it's terminal?"

"Noah's fine," I assure her.

"Stay out of this, Gabby," Britta warns, not taking her eyes off me. "I'm trying to have a serious conversation with my cousin."

"I'm done talking to you," I tell her, giving a dismissive wave. "Whatever you're trying to prove—"

Noah's chuckle fills the room as he breezes in through the doorway. "Didn't realize I'd be crashing a going away party." He gathers me inside his arms and gives me a sultry kiss. "You almost ready, sweetheart?"

"We're helping your bride decide what to bring," Gabby explains, her tone light and playful. "She's a bit overwhelmed by your generous gift, *Romeo*. A girl needs more time to prepare for two weeks in paradise."

She carefully sets the selection of jewelry on the bed next to the dresses before her collagen-filled lips form a complete circle. "Oooo, I have one of those chain-link, gold chokers that would look amazing with that green dress. Hold on, I'll be back in a jiffy." She pats my arm and gives Noah's cheek a playful pinch before whisking away.

"Enough with the packing," Noah tells me, his whiskey-colored eyes alight with mischief. "I can buy you anything you need once we're there." With his arms still wrapped around me, he sways like we're dancing. "Then again, I'd prefer to spend the next fifteen days with my gorgeous wife completely naked."

"I have to go," Britta announces, spinning toward the door. She pauses to grip the threshold, giving us only somewhat of a sincere smile. "Have a wonderful trip, you two." Her gaze lingers on mine, silently asking me to consider her accusation. "If you grow tired of him ravaging you twenty-four/seven and need some girl time, I'm only a phone call away."

"I can't imagine I'd ever tire of this beautiful man ravaging me," I reply, my voice sharper than intended. Looking into Noah's gaze, I grin. "In fact, I don't think I can wait until we arrive in St. Thomas. Good thing you booked a private jet. I've always wanted to join the Mile High Club."

Noah's clearly stunned when I grab either side of his collar and drag him close for another passionate kiss. He doesn't respond at first and almost acts as if he can't catch his breath. I'm usually not this forward, but something is driving me to put on a show in front of my cousin.

By the time I pull away, Britta's gone.

———

After we've settled into the 5-bedroom villa in St. Thomas with sweeping views of Charlotte Amalie and its pristine turquoise water dotted with sailboats beneath sprawling cliffs, Noah instructs the 3-person staff to head into town with a long list of supplies.

We proceed to christen every luxurious bed before ending up in the master suite with French doors leading onto a generous deck that provides breath-taking views. We even make love on the wicker patio furniture on the deck before our hour-long tryst finally ends.

We crawl into the 4-poster bed afterward, sharing the chilled bottle of champagne left by the staff. Noah dribbles the last of his champagne on my naked body, lapping it up with his tongue before grinning up at me. "What do you think, Mrs. Huisman? Did I do okay by choosing this place?"

"It's the very definition of paradise," I say with a contented sigh. Smiling, I run my fingers through his waves of lush hair. "Thank you, Mr. Huisman. You have no idea how badly I needed time away."

Frowning, he sets his champagne flute on the nightstand before settling in next to me and playing with a lock of my curls between his fingers. "What's going on, sweetheart? What was with the weirdness this morning when I walked in on you ladies packing?"

"I blame it on the champagne," I say, bashfully lowering my chin. "Britta has been a bit…I guess you could say *bitchy* with me. I think she's jealous of what you and I have."

"You're probably right, although I don't understand why she doesn't divorce Oliver once and for all and find someone to grow old with." With a long huff, he shakes his head. "That man was never right for her to begin with."

Irritation pricks my skin. "Exactly how long have you and Britta been such good friends?"

"I moved back to the lake for a brief time after separating from Kathy, my first wife. That's the summer Britta stayed with your grandma before she passed away. I ran into her a few times while she was around."

I'd always wondered if Britta had seen him while she was staying with our grandma. I was jealous she was there but not jealous enough to face Noah again. "What happened between you and Kathy?"

He forces out a breath. "Are we seriously going to

do this right after we've made love, while we're both naked?"

I roll my eyes and twist my hand, gesturing for him to continue.

Growling under his breath, he threads his hands through his hair and leans back onto a pillow, explaining his story to the ceiling. "I was young and immature when I married her, alright? I met her during my junior year at the School of Mines. She was waitressing at a bar in Golden and still lived at home. When we discussed my plans post-college, she realized she was without a plan and would be stuck with her parents without any kind of future.

"Next thing I knew, she was pregnant even though she was on the pill. By the time she faked a miscarriage—something her doctor confirmed when we went in for an ultrasound—I was relieved as hell. That's when I realized I never wanted kids. Despite her deceitful actions, I made the unwise decision to forgive her.

"It was evident that we were never compatible with each other. Not even remotely. She was reclusive and so odd that friends and family found it difficult to engage in conversation with her. Hell, she wasn't even attractive. The encounter that should've been a one-time thing ended up extending for an unexpectedly long period of time."

Sprawling myself over his chest, I shrug. "I've seen pictures of her online. I didn't think she was *ugly*. A little artificial, maybe, but I wouldn't say unattractive."

"She underwent numerous procedures after I was ordered to pay several hundred thousand in alimony. Trust me, you'd question my sanity if you saw pictures from our wedding."

Leaning in closer, he kisses the tip of my nose. "You've got nothing to worry about, sweetheart. I'd never been as happy as I was the day our divorce was official. And she has nothing on you. You're part of the reason I regretted marrying her to begin with."

I scrunch my nose. "How so?"

His eyes volley back and forth between mine. "Because I realized I was still in love with you." His lips curl with a kind of sad smile. "I always have been, Max. That's why I couldn't make either of my other marriages work. I was trying to satisfy a void only you could fill."

Despite being jealous that he was married to two other women and hung out with Britta, I openly swoon. If he's being truthful, he might possibly be the sweetest man alive. With tears in my eyes, I lean for another kiss.

We fool around for a while longer before making love again. Soon after, he falls asleep.

Having never enjoyed naps, I decide to stay awake until late evening. I unpack our suitcases into the 16-foot closet attached to the master bathroom. It's only slightly larger than the closet in our lake home, but the drawers are lined with luxurious velvet, the same deep shade of blue as the cloth hangers.

With everything put away, I take the time to explore the master bathroom. Encased in white marble, it mirrors the spa-like aesthetics of the super-sized kitchen and includes a 2-person spa tub that overlooks the bay.

The staff stocked the villa with fresh flowers before our arrival, including 3-dozen red roses in the bathroom that I assume are to add to a romantic soak. A large glass container with a pump contains enough bubble soap to have several daily baths during our extended visit.

Amid Noah's deep slumber, he calls out. He's typically not one to talk in his sleep, so I hurry back, worried something's wrong.

But he's still motionless on his back, eyes shifting around behind their closed lids.

As I creep in closer, he moans, much like he had earlier on the deck when he'd climaxed.

"Oh, baby, I like that," he calls, his voice deep and sexy. "Oh, *Beth*."

CHAPTER 16
PRESENT DAY

Detective Josephine Kelly

Still parked across the road from the Huisman's monstrosity of a home, I drop back against the driver seat of my sedan. I was certain Britta Baxter's classmate had been telling the truth about Noah Huisman having an intimate relationship with Britta when she was still a teenager. I suspect the relationship may have ended with her death. I'm also convinced Noah Huisman had been sleeping with Linda Boese.

While it would give Maxine Huisman a clear motive, my gut tells me Mrs. Huisman's reaction to the picture of Linda Boese had been complete shock rather than a well-rehearsed act. I'm willing to bet Mrs. Huisman knows about her husband's affair but is still having difficulty accepting it.

However, it's unusual that Maxine Huisman insists on preserving her deceased cousin's reputation as a beloved community member. Why does she feel obligated to continue with the facade? Is she in denial? Is she trying to paint her cousin in a positive light so no one suspects her husband could've been involved in her death? Even Taylor Baxter had plenty of negative things to say about her mother.

After speaking with Britta's next-door neighbors, the Lufts and the Hansens, I'm getting a better idea of the real woman behind the popular videos. Everyone from Britta's professional and social circles I spoke with at the memorial service sounded exasperated by Britta's antics. Not a single one seemed overly mournful of her death.

There seems to have been a darker side to the self-made celebrity than the carefully planned photographs posted online, intended to cast the influencer in a positive light.

Either Maxine Huisman was delusional in thinking her cousin was cherished by those who knew her, or she's hiding something.

Noah Huisman is good for the murders. I only have to unearth concrete evidence to back my theory and look into his alibi for the night of the murders. The task would become more difficult now that Mrs. Huisman wants a lawyer involved.

Remembering how Taylor Baxter had mentioned the Huismans' neighbor had also been a friend of her mother's, I exit my sedan a second time and start for the urban rambler a hundred feet from the Huismans' home.

When the zealous, buxom blonde answers the door, I sense I've struck gold. The woman all but hugs me and declares me to be her new best friend before she instructs me to make myself at home in the living room nearby. I take my time studying a wall of framed pictures, noting they almost all consist of selfies taken by Ms. Gallo with others. Although the house was designed with a minimalistic eye, the furnishings are clearly high-end, much like those inside the Husimans' home. Moments after the whistle of a tea kettle, I hear the click of Ms. Gallo's heels on the wood floor behind me.

"I'm so glad they put an intelligent woman in charge of this investigation," she declares while handing me a warm cup of chamomile tea. She glides away in a cloud of flowering fabric and bright patterns before claiming her spot in the opposing armchair. "God knows we don't need more arrogant men mucking things up. There are already too many ancient, wealthy white dudes running this country into the ground."

"Cheers to that." I raise my cup before taking a minuscule sip for show. "You have a lovely home. Have you been here long?"

"I just celebrated my first year of living here full-time. If it weren't for Britta and Maxine, I'd still be wasting most of my year away, slumming it in Palm Springs."

"You're from California?"

"Born and raised."

Eyebrows raised, I set the cup and saucer on the coffee table. "How did you find your way here?"

"It's a long story. I'd hate to bore you with the mundane details. In a nutshell, I'm a widow who has a string of terrible luck. My second late husband's family owned this property, so I sort of fell into it like a drunk would fall over a cobblestone street after too much Italian wine."

My professionalism kicks in, preventing me from openly laughing at the woman's oddities. "*Second* late husband?"

"Well, my first one, Tony, died because he was overweight and didn't bother listening when the doctor told him his heart would give out if he didn't stop stuffing his face."

"And how did your second husband pass away?"

Gabby's eyes narrow as if she's sharing something scandalous. "Paully was a *pill popper* who also had a passion for *fast muscle cars*. I think you can guess how he met his demise."

"I can't imagine that combo ended well."

"They had to cut out a portion of the brick wall he hit so they could test his brain matter for illegal substances."

I inwardly shudder at the visual. "They investigated his cause of death?"

"His father is a powerful man with a lot of enemies. He wanted to make certain someone hadn't put a hit out on his son." She holds her hand beside her mouth and adds, "He was a boss in the Italian mafia."

My eyebrows shoot up on their own. "Did they investigate your first husband's cause of death?"

Gabby's mouth puckers. "Are you suggesting I'm some kind of black widow?"

"I'm simply interested in the details of your 'string of terrible luck,' as you called it." Although I fully intend to research the stories of the two men, it's time for a change of subject before she becomes upset with me. "Tell me more about your relationship with the Huismans. You must witness plenty with all these open windows. Are you only close with

Maxine, or do you also have a relationship with Noah?"

Sitting a little taller, Gabby folds her hands in her lap. "I'm not going to sit here and pretend I don't find Noah hella sexy, but my relationship with him doesn't go beyond anything innocent. I'm not a harlot. And besides, I wouldn't do that sort of thing to my best friend. Max and I have each other's backs through thick and thin."

The irony of her mentioning "backs" when both women had been stabbed in theirs isn't lost on me. The widow may have a tendency towards murdering those who have done her wrong, including female friends and acquaintances. "I understand Britta and Maxine had a close-knit friendship as well as being cousins. Have you ever experienced jealousy towards their relationship?"

"Of course not. I felt lucky when they invited me into their circle."

"How did Britta and Maxine get along? Were you aware of any rivalry between them? Any old, unsettled riffs?"

"You're asking if I think my sweet friend killed her beloved cousin and tossed her corpse into the lake because of some old grudge? The answer is *hell* to the *no*." Her cheeks flush with anger. "You didn't witness

Maxine falling apart after they stuck Brit's body inside the hearse. Her cousin's death *destroyed* her. She's been walking around like some kinda zombie!"

"Okay, okay," I concede, holding up the palms of my hands in a peaceful gesture. "I'm trying to do a thorough job. Let's go back to Mr. Huisman. Do you have any reason to believe he's been unfaithful to his wife, either recently or in the past?"

"That's not for me to say," she says, again folding her hands against her lap. "I, for one, don't engage in small-town gossip."

Sensing she's eager to tell me something, I pretend to be satisfied with the answer by saying, "I can respect that."

Gabby leans closer and whispers, "But if I tell you a secret, can you promise it won't get back to Max?"

I nod, waiting for her to continue.

"Everyone around here considers Noah Huisman to be a total player. They laughed behind Max's back when word got around they were getting married after only a few months. I mean, the man has been married two times before. Did she really believe another worthless piece of paper would make him a loyal husband?"

"From what I understand, he's out of town quite often. Do you believe he's unfaithful while he's away?"

Gabby scoffs. "I mean, come on. Did you get a proper look at the man? He was put on this earth to seduce women."

"Would it surprise you to learn he'd been intimate with Britta Baxter?"

Gabby's eyes flicker over to the Huismans' home, visible through a large set of square windows. A bank of clouds has moved in over the fortress-sized home, giving it a more sinister vibe.

"Real talk...just between us girls?" Gabby offers, her voice hardly a step above a whisper. "Not at all. Britta and Noah were like the real-life Ken and Barbie of Lake Shetek. I mean, they're so attractive and perfect. The rest of us should be embarrassed. Max is beautiful and everything, but she's more of a natural beauty, kinda like Day to Night Barbie with the pink suit and the sensible pumps, while Britta was a total Crystal Barbie...all glitter and glamour. I mean, all Barbies are plastic, so it might not be the best comparison. At least as far as Max is concerned. Know what I mean?"

Although a little confused by the odd metaphors, I nod regardless. "Did you know Linda Boese?"

"Is that the dead girl Donna Rivers found yesterday?" Gabby's eyes begin to sparkle with unshed tears. "Poor thing. I've seen her at the bar a handful of times. She was *beautiful*. She had so much to offer.

Just think of the superb babies she could've brought into the world had she found the right man. What kind of sicko would want to wipe someone with so much potential off the face of this earth?"

"Miss Boese's twin sister suspects Linda was having an affair with a man from this area," I say, careful to gauge the movement of every muscle on the woman's body.

Eyes widening, Gabby slaps her knees. "Wait. Is that why you had all those questions about Noah? Do you think he was sleeping with Britta *and* the hot bartender?"

"I'm searching for any facts about the area's two recent victims that will lead to an arrest."

Gabby gasps. "So you think the two deaths were related? What if some psychopath serial killer on this lake has a thing for hot blondes?" Her shaking hands flutter over the sides of her face. "Oh no! What if they come after me next?"

"At this point in time, we don't have reason to believe more murders will occur, but as always, it doesn't hurt to err on the side of caution. Don't go out alone at night, keep your doors and windows locked at all times. If you have reason to believe you're in danger, don't hesitate to call nine-one-one."

"It's a good thing I got my conceal and carry when I first moved here," Gabby says with a tisk. "A young, single, vulnerable woman like me can never be too careful."

I balk at the idea of the eccentric woman handling a firearm. *God help us all.* "Like I said, call nine-one-one if you think you might be in danger." Standing, I pass my business cards to the woman. "Please don't hesitate to reach out if you can think of anything helpful."

"Oh, I will," Gabby promises with an enthusiastic nod. "You can count on it."

And you can count on the fact that I will learn what exactly happened to your husbands by the day's end, I silently add.

CHAPTER 17
PRESENT DAY

Maxine

After camping out in the hidden pantry, watching out the window until I'm certain Detective Kelly has finally left Gabby's house and the neighborhood, I spend a few minutes hunched over the toilet.

What if the man I promised to spend the rest of my life with is a murderer?

As much as I want to deny it, how can it be a coincidence I found a picture of the woman on his phone mere hours before she washed up on the lakeshore?

I flush the toilet and rinse my mouth before

rushing into our closet. I start with Noah's bank of drawers, tossing everything aside into a heaping pile on the tiled floor. I honestly have no idea what I'm looking for or what I'm trying to prove. I'm on autopilot as I empty the entire contents of his side of the U-shaped closet.

From there, I head into his office on the second floor, dumping out each drawer to frantically search for hidden compartments. Somewhere in the back of my mind, I acknowledge my neat husband will be livid when he discovers the mess I've made of his important documents. I'm past the point of caring.

I make my way through the house one room at a time. At this point, I'm sure I've completely lost my mind. But I need something to either confirm my greatest fears or negate them. There's no in-between.

Once I've finished combing through every square inch, I stare at the doorway tucked in the back of the pantry. When the house was first built, Noah left the basement unfinished. According to him, he had a fall out with the architect over something to do with the layout of the wine cellar. Although he ultimately decided to leave it until he could find an architect who shared his vision, there's still a makeshift room dry and cool enough to store the cases of wine he brings home from every business trip.

I rarely go into the room as it houses numerous

spiders of different varieties, no matter how many times the exterminators come to spray. I usually either make Noah retrieve the bottle of wine I want if he's home, or I run into town and buy whatever is needed to pair with dinner. I prefer not to step foot into the dark cellar at any cost. So when I think about it, it's the perfect place for Noah to hide something from me.

Taking a deep breath for courage, I pad barefoot down the stairway, finished in the same white oak as the other stairways in the house. As I flip on the light switch, my pulse dances to an erratic beat. Under the golden glow of oversized construction lightbulbs dangling from the ceiling, the barren cement space comes to life.

Although it's been three years since the contractor finished taping the ceiling and gave it a coat of primer, the "new construction" smell remains prominent as I shuffle through the empty space.

The cold concrete on my bare feet evokes memories of a disturbing occurrence from my childhood. It comes hard and unexpectedly, forcing me to lean against the nearest wall to stay upright.

I was sure the memory of that horrific day had remained buried.

• • •

My mom's boyfriend, Martin, came to our house every Sunday afternoon without fail. He was a traditional Southern Baptist and never missed a Sunday morning service. He'd force me to pray for salvation on my knees at his side, often for several hours. My little legs and joints would lock up so I couldn't walk for several minutes after he finally permitted me to stand.

Once, when I was six, I wet myself because he wouldn't let me use the bathroom. After that incident, I learned to empty my bladder minutes before he would arrive.

My mother was conveniently absent during these prayer sessions involving what could only be described as acts of torture. She'd show up around dinnertime to prepare something fresh from the supermarket, pretending nothing nefarious happened while she was away.

One Sunday afternoon, days after my thirteenth birthday, I decided I'd had enough of Martin's prayer sessions. My mother left early, leaving me alone nearly ten minutes before his scheduled arrival. I crawled under the house's concrete foundation to hide. The space was tight and filled with some of Georgia's least-desired creatures, but I didn't care. It was safer than being at Martin's disposal.

My plan would've worked if I hadn't come face-to-face with a copperhead snake.

I actually willed the snake to bite me.

I closed my eyes and prayed it would end my life,

prayed it would stop the misery I had to endure over and over again.

My prayers were answered as Martin stepped out of his vehicle in the driveway. I gave my hiding spot away with a wail of pure agony.

Five bags of anti-venom were necessary to keep me alive. Without them, a surgeon would've amputated my leg. My mother was unaccounted for in the two days I spent in the ICU. Martin told the hospital staff he was my father, so they allowed him to stay. Unfortunately, he remained vigilant at my side.

Despite the narcotics they continuously pumped into me, hoping to take the edge off, I'd never understood that level of suffering.

It was still better than the fate awaiting me once I was released.

One late evening during my stay in the hospital, when Martin was asleep, I tried to tell one of the young nurses why I didn't want to go home. Either Martin wasn't really sleeping, or he woke at the very start of the conversation. He told the nurse I wasn't right in the head, and they continued the conversation in the hallway.

The thing about Martin was he knew how to charm anyone. I guess women who didn't understand he was evil found him attractive. The next time I saw that nurse, she *was flirting with him and blushing at almost everything he said.*

In that hospital bed, I started planning my escape.

The flashback sends a jolt to my system, almost knocking me off my feet. I've tried to suppress any memories involving Martin for so long.

Now I understand why I've done everything to avoid this basement.

With a guttural cry, I sink to the floor.

I was so young, so innocent. What kind of a monster does countless evil things to a child? And how did my mother stand by all those years without stopping him?

You've come this far, Maxine. Don't let that bastard break you now.

I wipe my wet face and stand, continuing toward the makeshift cellar. Dozens of bottles rest on the custom racks, half covered in a layer of dust. I peruse through the meticulously arranged selections, curious how many thousands of dollars Noah has dropped on alcohol that may or may not ever be consumed.

At this point, I'm half tempted to open the most expensive bottle I can find and wallow in my sorrows until I procure a Plan B. But I need to keep my wits about me, especially if I'm going to clean up the mess I made upstairs before Noah returns. *If* he returns, I remind myself. I've lost track of his schedule.

En route back to the stairway, I glance up at the nearest oversized lightbulb hanging from wires. A black handle peers out from the hole cut in the drywall by the contractors for a light box. I drag an empty crate over from the corner and teeter on my tiptoes to reach the object.

It's a knife.

It could be a drywall tool the contractor left behind. However, by the size of it, I suspect it's a chef's knife.

With a rush of bone-rattling chills, I study it inside my open hand. Although it doesn't match the set of professional-grade stainless steel knives we'd registered for with the rest of our wedding presents, it's unquestionably a high-quality knife.

Rocked by a memory, I waver on my feet.

The morning after Britta's death, I'd made Taylor her favorite eggs cooked in bacon grease.

When I had reached for a knife in Britta's butcher block, I noticed one of the slots were empty.

The set was black.

The knife is from Britta's kitchen.

———

In the next blink of my eyes, I'm sitting at our kitchen island.

Gabby grips my forearms, shaking me.

As I look around, my eyelids feel heavy, as if they are covered in lead. "What's going on?" I mumble. "What happened?"

Gabby crushes me into her arms. "Oh, thank god! For a moment, I was afraid I would have to slap you silly, and I didn't want to have to do you dirty like that. You were sitting there like a total space cadet, staring out the window."

When she draws back, I glance around the house. It's dark out. What time did I go into the basement? It must've been long before noon.

"How did I get up here?" I whisper. The last thing I remember, I'd found the knife tucked inside the basement ceiling. I must've blacked out after. Cold fear winds a ribbon around my heart. *Where'd the knife go?*

Gabby frowns down on me. "Where were you before?"

"Never mind," I say, pushing away from the island to slide off the stool.

"I like what you've done with the place," Gabby sniggers. She motions to the emptied cupboards situated near the back entrance. "What happened here,

Max? Did you have some kind of adverse reaction to those benzos I gave you?"

"I think Noah was having an affair," I blurt.

Gabby's threaded eyebrows shoot up to her hairline. "And you thought you might find the little hussy hiding in your cupboards?"

"I was hoping I'd come across something to vindicate him." Remembering the knife, my stomach heaves. Fortunately, I didn't eat anything all day. Or at least I *think* I didn't. "What time is it?"

"It's almost eight." Her augmented lips tremble with anger. "Are you expecting the cheating bastard to come home tonight?"

"No…I mean…I guess I don't know."

How did I lose track of an entire day? I've experienced time lapses before, but never for more than a handful of hours. If Gabby wasn't doting on me, I would sneak out to the garage and see if my car's engine was warm. What did I spend the day doing?

"Max, babe, I'm worried about you. No offense, but you look like roadkill baked in the sun for a week." Concern darkens her gaze. "What makes you believe Noah had an affair?"

"I found a picture of a topless woman on his phone. He tried to delete it, but he must not know deleted pictures don't immediately disappear."

"I'm sure it was just some porn he downloaded

from the internet," Gabby offers, heading over to the bar area. "How about I pour you a drink? You look like you could use a stiff one."

Irritation growing, I wipe both hands over my face. I need a minute alone to piece together the last several hours of my life and decide what to do about the discovery of what I think to be Britta's knife.

Gabby has proven to be a fiercely loyal friend. I wouldn't be surprised if she would volunteer to help me dispose of the evidence to prevent my husband from spending the rest of his life behind bars. But I also don't want her getting too involved until Noah's intentions are clear.

What if killing Britta and the waitress made him thirsty for more blood? I might be in danger of becoming his next victim.

I wipe at my brow, feigning dizziness. "You know, I'm not feeling the best, Gabs. I think I'm going to lie down."

"Would you rather I make you a cup of chamomile tea?"

I flash an appreciative smile. "Thank you for offering, but I need some peace and quiet. I'm sure I can sleep off whatever this is. I'll talk to you tomorrow."

As I'm beginning to turn away from her, she blurts, "Max, wait! Does this have anything to do with the pretty bartender they found? Do you think Noah might've been sleeping with her?"

When our eyes meet, I struggle to come up with an answer. She already knows the truth. She'll see right through anything I say, any lie I come up with.

With a solemn nod, she gestures towards the kitchen island. "Sit down, sister. I'll pour us some strong drinks. Sounds like you're gonna need one."

CHAPTER 18
9 MONTHS EARLIER

Maxine

In a rare gesture of hospitality, Britta invites Noah and me over for dinner one night. Typically, such an invitation would only be extended to Gabby and me.

Maybe she's ready to apologize for accusing Noah of cheating before we left for St. Thomas. Maybe she noticed our equally tanned faces and satisfied smiles, and decided I wouldn't entertain her wild notions a second time.

She was unaware I knew about Beth. And I wasn't about to clue her in.

When we walk in on Oliver pouring wine in the

kitchen, Noah grips my forearm as I trip over my feet.

"Oliver." I choke down a startled squeal. "I can't believe you're here." I don't bother sugarcoating my surprise with any pleasantries. Everyone in the room knows my disdain for my cousin's estranged husband.

"It's my house, too," he reminds me.

I openly roll my eyes and accept the glass of wine he offers. "I wasn't aware."

Britta steps in beside him in her favorite bright red apron over a black cocktail dress almost identical to mine. "The side dishes will be ready in half an hour." She clinks one of the other full glasses against mine. "It's our job to get properly drunk while the men cook the steaks."

"On it," Oliver tells her with an oddly compliant nod. "Come on, Noah. I've got a couple of cigars and glasses of bourbon waiting out by the grill."

Noah bends to kiss me. "For the record, I'd rather hang out with you," he whispers into my ear before trailing after Oliver.

Britta and I sip our wine until the French doors close behind them.

"What gives?" I spin on my heels to confront her head-on. "Why does it feel like we've walked into an episode of *The Twilight Zone*? Have you two made amends or something?"

"Even better." Britta's lips bend with a devilish smirk. "I may have talked him into filing for a divorce."

"How?" I challenge, doubting it to be true.

"I can't say for sure. Maybe he's sick of pretending like I am. Maybe he's found someone that makes it easier to move on."

"How will you divide your assets?"

Her smirk fades away. "We haven't made it that far into the conversation. I hope he'll be a reasonable adult when the time comes."

"Britta, that's the reason you've stayed married this long. What makes you think he's going to suddenly be a bigger person and agree to a fair split?"

"I don't know," she admits, dropping her shoulders. "But I'm sick of living like this. I'm ready to move on...find the person I was truly meant to grow old with. You know?"

Suspicion flickers through my mind. *Funny, Noah had just said something very similar while in St. Thomas.*

All at once, there's a commotion outside. Patio furniture flies past the French doors.

"You're a goddamn liar!" Oliver roars.

Britta and I exchange wide-eyed glances before

darting out to the patio. By the time we reach Oliver and Noah, they're twisted around each other on the deck floor, determined fists swinging through the air.

"Noah, stop!" I cry, unwilling to throw myself into the violent exchange to separate them. "What are you doing?"

Oliver lands an experienced right hook into Noah's face. Noah roars, cradling his nose, as Oliver backs off, cradling his hand.

"Enough!" Britta demands, yanking on her husband's collar to pull him away.

"You broke my nose!" Noah snarls at Oliver before spitting a mouthful of blood.

"You're lucky that's all I broke!" Oliver fires back.

"Come on," I tell Noah, hooking my arm underneath his armpits to help him stand. "We're going home."

Britta backs away from her husband. "Maybe you two should talk—"

"I've had enough talking with this imbecile," Oliver tells her, stomping into the house.

We all watch as he cuts through the house to the door leading into the garage. A moment later, the metal garage door whirls open, followed an engine roar and tires squealing.

Britta rolls her eyes. "Sometimes he acts like a damn teenager." She sets a hand on the crook of

Noah's arm. "Are you alright? You should go to the ER and have that looked at."

"I'm fine," he insists, jerking away from her. "I broke my nose a bunch of times in football. My mom taught me how to reset it." He presses on either side of his nose and inhales deeply before jerking his hands to the left. I wince with the quiet crack that follows.

I eye Britta with growing suspicion. "Aren't you going to ask what their argument was about?"

She flinches and side-eyes Noah. "Whatever it was doesn't matter. I'm sure Oliver's immaturity unnecessarily escalated the situation."

Noah tugs on my hand. "Let's go."

Britta's silent as we leave.

On the boat ride back, Noah stares into the darkness with an alarming amount of intensity. I purposely don't question him.

I want his full attention when the inevitable argument begins.

Once inside our kitchen, he pours a full glass of whiskey over ice before taking the remainder of the bottle to the island. I rummage through the freezer for a bag of peas and hand it over.

"Put this over your nose and left eye. You're gonna have a nice shiner in the morning."

"Thanks," he grumbles, snatching it from my

hold. He gingerly places it against his nose and hisses. "I hope that asshole broke his hand."

"He took boxing in college, Noah. He knows how to throw a punch without injuring himself." I take the bag and shift it to partially cover his bruised eye. "What did you two argue about?"

"I asked when he was finally going to let Britta go."

"Doesn't explain why he called you a liar," I point out.

Snatching the bag from me, he tosses it onto the island. "Can we do this another time? I'm beginning to get a whale of a headache."

"I'll grab you some painkillers after you tell me one thing." I clench my fists against my thighs. "Is it over between you and Britta?"

Glancing at the ceiling, he holds his arms out. "Christ, Max! I told you—"

"No more lying," I snarl. "I want to know the truth! Why are you and Britta both so intent on lying about it when I *know* you've slept together?"

"How in the hell could you possibly know such a thing?"

"Are you afraid to admit it because you were still legally married to Kathy at the time? You said you were separated when you first came back here. If you're worried it's because I'll suspect you're a serial cheater—"

His eyes harden with resolve. "I would *never* be unfaithful to you, Max."

"Dammit, Noah! Tell me the truth, or I'm walking out the door and never coming back!"

"Alright!" he concedes, holding the palms of his hands up. "I'll tell you!" Turning away, he swipes his full glass off the island, chugging it in one gulp. He then slams the empty glass down, licks his lips, and takes a deep breath. "Britta and I don't admit we slept together because we have an agreement that affects more than just the two of us."

"I don't understand."

"Remember how I said I'd realized I didn't want children after Kathy faked her pregnancy?"

"Of course." I wind my arms around myself. "That was a memorable conversation."

"I was mad at Kathy and in a bad headspace when Britta came here that first summer to stay with your grandma. When I ran into her, it took a minute to register it was your cousin. She was so much older than the scrawny kid you brought to my house that one New Year's. I know this will sound messed up, but being around your cousin made me feel closer to you."

"You're right," I say, flashing the palm of one hand. "That's extremely messed up."

"Well, I must've been blitzed out of my mind by the end of that night because I don't remember hooking up with her until I found her naked in my bed the next morning."

I grimace. "I don't need to know the details."

"I want to clarify that I wasn't in my right mind. Because I missed you so damn much, and she reminded me of you, I must've drank myself stupid."

"You're five years older than Britta," I say as if he needed reminding after the fact. "How old was she?"

His eyes briefly close. "Seventeen."

Acid rises in my throat. While I'm confident nearly every state in the US has deemed the age of consent to be either 16 or 17, I'm also aware that doesn't necessarily mean it would've been legal for a young adult to have sex with a minor. "You don't want anyone knowing, including me, because she was under eighteen? She would've turned eighteen before fall."

"It's a bit more complicated than that." He refills his glass and takes a large swallow. "We didn't see each other again the entire first year she was at the U. When she returned the following summer, she wanted to hook up again."

With a grunt, I swipe the glass from his hand and

suck down the remainder. Unsurprisingly, the sting of the bitter alcohol doesn't do anything to tame the acid burning through my esophagus. Once Britta started college, we hung out quite often. She was spending entire weekends at my apartment in St. Paul.

"I tried to convince her that she should find someone her age," Noah continues. "I told her she would be better off with someone she could marry and start a family with since those weren't things I wanted. When we ran into each other at the street dance the night before the Fourth of July, she tried to kiss me. I told her I was done and it would never happen again.

"Mid-August of that year, she stopped by my place with a bottle of tequila. She was determined to convince me it wouldn't be so bad marrying her and having her children. Even though I was freaked out and wanted her to leave, I must've blacked out from the tequila. I don't know how to explain it...being around her made me crazy in a bad way. I hardly remember a single detail of those two nights after a certain point. It's like I couldn't drink enough when she was around. It's a lame as hell excuse, but it's true."

He pauses, watching the ice jingle in his hand. "The first time we slept together, there was a condom wrapper on the nightstand. The second time..." Anger flickers through his eyes when he gulps down the rest of his drink.

Numbness creeps into my veins. I know what he's trying to say long before the words spill from his lips.

"Two weeks after she returned to college, she called to let me know she'd taken a pregnancy test." His bloodshot gaze returns to me. "Taylor's mine."

CHAPTER 19
PRESENT DAY

Maxine

Once Noah calls to let me know he'll be spending another night in the cities and will return the following evening, Gabby and I stay up until early morning. While she does her part to empty our wine cellar, I review my knowledge of Noah's history with Britta and fill her in on the knife I discovered.

We both stare at Britta's house through the bay windows as if waiting for her to return home. I've become accustomed to seeing it dark all the time. At this early hour, before the sun has yet to rise, it projects an eerie darkness.

"Before we jump to any conclusions and assume he's guilty of something this extreme, we need to gather more evidence," Gabby decides, tapping her sharp nails against her umpteenth glass of red wine. "It's pretty clear he had a hand in Brit's death, but why?"

"Maybe they didn't stop seeing each other after Taylor was born," I grumble, swirling my untouched wine. "They could've already been together when he suggested I move back. That day, when we ran into him on the beach, she acted like she *owned* him. And on our first anniversary, she tried convincing me he was cheating on me." Without question, she's jealous of what Noah and I have. My heart gives a little squeeze. "Probably because he refused to commit to her like he did to me."

Gabby nods enthusiastically. "And she was getting ready to spill the beans to you, so he silenced her! That would make perfect sense! Now we just need to somehow confirm he was seeing that bartender!"

Letting out a curt laugh, I guzzle more wine. "You don't think that nude selfie was proof enough?"

"Sorry to be the one to tell you this, sister, but I'm sure your hot hubby has a harem of women throwing themselves at him every time he's in New York. And around here, an attractive man of his caliber is a rarity. Especially when you add in the rich factor."

She turns to me, her eyes narrowed into slits. "You know, that detective mentioned Linda Boese has a twin sister. We could find out where she lives and invite her over so she's here when Noah arrives. If he killed that woman, I imagine it would shake him up to see her doppelgänger sitting in his home."

"That wouldn't be such a bad idea," I half-heartedly agree. Although I haven't had as much to drink as Gabby, delirium—I imagine from a lack of sleep—is setting in. "First, we'd have to find out if they're actually identical. Otherwise, it won't work."

"You can tell him you invited her over for coffee because you understood what she was going through after you lost Britta. Having to come face-to-face with his victim's sister would likely make him uncomfortable, even if they're not identical."

"I guess you're right."

Gabby lifts her phone from the island and begins swiping a finger over the screen. "Hold on, I bet I can find the answer in under thirty seconds. As much as I hate all the negativity and nonsense of social media, it sure comes in handy for unexpected reasons."

She concentrates harder, sticking her tongue out as she finishes typing. A moment later, she beams proudly when showing me her phone's screen.

"Voila! You don't need a DNA test to prove they're identical!"

In Molly Boese's profile picture, two blonde women in matching cowboy hats and low-cut T-shirts embrace in front of an outdoor stage where a band performs, each grinning from ear to ear.

They're a mirror image.

———

I sleep until early afternoon, then drag myself out of bed and get ready like any other morning. Although inebriated when she left, Gabby promised to track Molly Boese down this morning and bring her by as soon possible—assuming she's in town because of her sister's death.

I spend the next hour putting Noah's belongings away, only somewhat worried I'm doing something wrong that will make him suspicious. At some point in time, I'll have to confront him about the knife, even if it breaks my heart to think he would be capable of killing someone I loved.

As I wait for a second pot of coffee to brew, the doorbell chimes.

Gabby and an exact replica of the topless woman stand on my front step. The young woman is short and petite with a remarkably smaller chest than her twin's. Her gray "Johnny Cash" T-shirt and jean shorts are modest, and her sunny blond hair is pulled into a high ponytail. She wears bright white sneakers and a fashionable sling purse. Mild puffiness beneath her sapphire-colored eyes makes me wonder if she'd been crying on the way here.

Red-hot jealousy clogs my throat. She's so young and...*perky*. Is she Noah's new type?

Gabby motions to the woman. "Max, this is Molly. Her sister's the one they found in the lake...like your cousin."

"I'm sorry for your loss," I offer, swinging the door open. "Come on in. I'll have coffee for anyone who wants it in a minute. Otherwise, I have water and soda, too."

"I'm okay," Molly mumbles, entering ahead of Gabby.

Gabby and I exchange a tense look.

Molly slowly spins around beneath the grand windows overlooking the lake. "This place is really something. I always wondered what it was like inside."

"Thank you." I motion to the couch. "Go ahead and have a seat."

"On second thought," she says, wearily eyeing the couch, "do you have the stuff to make a Bloody Mary?"

I start for the built-in bar across the kitchen. "I'm pretty sure I do."

"I'll take one too!" Gabby calls after me.

"How did you know my sister again?" Molly asks as I'm filling a glass with ice.

"She served me at the Legion a few times," Gabby answers. "It's not like we were besties or anything. Was she married? Did she have kids?"

"No kids or husband…only a boyfriend," Molly offers.

Gabby's voice raises an octave. "Someone from around here?"

"I guess. I live in the cities and hadn't been back in a while, so I never got to meet him."

After pouring the vodka, I turn back to join the conversation. "We might know him. What was his name?"

Still standing in the center of the living room, she shrugs. "She never told me."

"Do you think it was because he was married?" Gabby presses a little too eagerly.

"What's going on here?" Molly blurts, side-eying us both. "Did you two bring me here so you could find out the scoop on my sister's affair with a married man? Was she sleeping with one of your husbands? Is that it?"

Gabby throws me a cautious glance.

"We simply feel bad for you, having lost your sister," I explain with a gentle smile. "My cousin was like a sister to me, too. We thought it would help if you and I met so we could grieve together."

"Bullshit." Molly's smooth, blemish-free face flushes with anger. "How dare you play stupid games with someone in mourning—"

"You're right," I admit, fearful she'll take off. "I have reason to believe my husband was having an affair with your sister."

Her glare on me feels murderous. "Do the police know that?"

"I think, at this point, Detective Kelly suspects it to be true," Gabby replies on my behalf. "We don't have any hard proof at this point."

"Has she questioned him about it?"

I shake my head. "I love my husband, and I don't think he's capable of murder," I explain with tears building behind my eyes. "I don't want to throw him under the bus if he didn't kill her. I won't get him involved as a suspect unless I have something to prove his guilt."

Gabby and I agreed it isn't necessary to tell her about the knife. At least not yet.

"What do you want from me?" she asks, spreading her arms wide. "I already told you I had no idea what he looks like."

"It doesn't matter," Gabby explains. "We're hoping we can gauge his reaction by having you approach him when he returns...make him think he's being haunted."

Molly lets out a harsh laugh. "Men like him are skilled liars. What makes you think he won't act perfectly normal when he sees me, even if he did it?" Staring at the floor, she shakes her head. "Besides, a reaction isn't actual proof of anything."

"I might have another idea," Gabby tells her, glancing in my direction. "Didn't you tell me Noah has an aversion to sleeping pills?"

I throw her a half-hearted shrug. "Yeah...he becomes loopy and sometimes a little over-emotional before passing out cold."

Turning back to Molly, she tilts her head. "How are your acting skills?"

CHAPTER 20
PRESENT DAY

Beth

Noah's still away on business when I call Taylor. I haven't checked in on her since her momma died. I need to confirm she's okay and thrivin'. If my idea of what to do with Noah goes down as planned, there's a chance it could get messy. It's possible I may never see her again.

"Hey!" she shouts over the crass beat of hard rock and laughter blastin' in the background. "You caught me in the middle of planning Payton's bachelor party with the best man. We're at a bar in Midtown…it's pretty loud here. Can I call you back?"

"Actually, this can't wait," I say. "It's important. Can you step outside for a minute?"

"Yeah, sure." After a minute passes, the music becomes muffled. "Okay, you have my full attention. It's raining, so I'm in the bathroom. What's up?"

"It's about your *real* father," I begin, attemptin' to keep hatred from seepin' into my voice. "Noah."

"What *about* him?" she snaps. "I already told you I want nothing to do with him. *Or* Oliver. They're both dead to me."

"I understand why you're upset with Oliver, but he was told the truth only a short time before you. Your momma and Noah kept it a secret from everyone until recently. Oliver was convinced they were lyin' until he sent the DNA test."

Taylor lets out a long sigh. "I should hate my mom for hiding the truth my whole life, but it's hard to hold a grudge against someone who's gone. You know what I mean?"

"It's still okay to hate her. You certainly wouldn't be the only one."

She giggles. "You sound funny. Are you okay?"

"I'm fine, but I'm callin' to remind you of somethin' important. If anythin' were to happen to your biological father, you'd be entitled to a portion of his estate. And I can assure you, Noah's filthy rich."

"You think I care about that douche-bag's money?" she replies with a sarcastic laugh. "You said he made my mom lie to my dad because he didn't want me. Between my career and the money Mom left me as a safety net, I'm set. They can bury him with my inheritance. Better yet, I'll take it and give it all to charity. Plenty of kids in the system would benefit from having a college scholarship waiting for them when they turn eighteen. Like you've always said—kids from bad families just need a break in life, right?"

"You're a sweet girl with a pure heart, Tay. Payton will be the luckiest man alive to have you as his wife."

"Are you sure you're okay? You hardly ever call me 'Tay'."

Glancin' up at the house Noah poured an exuberant amount of money into, I pause to light a cigarette and take a long, satisfyin' drag.

The nightmare will be over soon.

"I'm more than okay, darlin'."

"Okay, *weirdo*." The tinklin' laugh she lets out makes me grin. "Why are you acting like this conversation is urgent?"

"I have a good feelin' Noah will be arrested for the murder of your momma."

Other than the muted sounds of the bar's music, my revelation is met with silence.

"Taylor, did you hear me?"

"Yeah, I heard you." She sniffles. "Do you think he did it?"

"Oh, baby girl, I *know* he did."

CHAPTER 21
28 YEARS EARLIER

Noah

I finally convince Max to stay in Minnesota for the summer. With the old beater my folks gave me for making the A honor roll every semester last year, I drive her and her grandma to the hospital in Worthington for her grandma's chemotherapy treatments.

I also take Max back and forth to waitress in Slayton. Somehow, she claims she can make ends meet without needing money from her grandma. In whatever free time she has left, I'm usually at her grandma's trailer house on the lake. My mom sends dinner along with me so Max doesn't have the extra financial burden of food.

My sister and my mom have possibly fallen more in love with her than I have, which sometimes irritates the hell out of me. Other times, it kinda warms my heart. It's like she's a part of our family. And I like that. A lot.

Best of all, I like knowing she's safe when she's with us.

One hot night in July, I snag a bottle of my mom's wine when she isn't looking and drive Max to the State Park. We settle on a blanket in an isolated spot far from the other campers, and I encircle my arms around her as lightning bugs dance above the grass.

The dark sky's clear, allowing us to make out every constellation—at least the ones we know. The hazy, purple band of the Milky Way slices through the middle like the sky's cracking open. I've never seen Lake Shetek look so cool.

On my old man's portable boom box, I play a CD I burned with some of Max's favorite tunes. When Kurt Cobain's raspy voice begins to croon a remake of the old Beetles song, "And I Love Her"—a bootleg version I scored from an older cousin in Washington —Max sighs wearily.

"He had such a beautiful voice. I still can't believe he's gone."

Clearing my throat, I squeeze my arms around her. Since I'm afraid to tell her how much I love her after the last time, I decided to let Kurt speak for me. "This song…it makes me think of you."

Nudging my arms away, she spins around to straddle my lap. Her body's so soft and warm that I'm terrified I'll embarrass myself. My eyes dart over her shoulder as I try like hell to focus on the sounds of chirping frogs and water lapping the rocky shoreline. Anything to distract my body from ruining the moment.

But I can't force myself to ignore her for long. She's beyond beautiful in the pale moonlight cutting through the oak trees above us.

The gold flecks in her hazel eyes dance in the moonlight as she drags her fingers through my hair with a thoughtful smile. "Why are you so good to me?"

"Because I care about you…more than anything or anyone." I brush one of my thumbs over her soft, beautiful lips. "I love you, Max. I'd do anything to protect you."

Eyes shining with tears, she bends to press her lips against mine, surprising me with the sweep of her tongue. Until now, our kisses have been PG because I've always followed her lead. I hesitate to respond when she deepens the kiss and yanks my T-shirt upward.

I gently push her back. "You're tipsy. We should wait until you have a clear head."

"I know what I'm doing," she insists, pulling her dress over her head.

My entire body flushes warm with the sight of her white cotton underwear on her thin legs and breasts cradled inside a plain white bra. "Maybe we should talk about it, Max. I mean…you know…the thing that—"

"Make love to me, Noah," she pleads in the sweetest voice I've ever heard. She reaches for the front clasp on her bra. "I wanna know what it's supposed to feel like."

My throat thickens. "Are you sure?"

When her bra snaps open, she sucks her bottom lip into her mouth and nods. "I think the wine gave me the courage to finally tell you what I want. This… with you…I want it. I want *you*."

"I don't want to hurt you," I whisper, gripping her waist.

"You won't," she whispers back with a growing smile. With tears springing to her eyes, she takes my face inside her hands. "You're the only one in my life who's ever shown me what it's like to be loved, Noah."

Together, we tug my shirt over my head before we resume making out. Once we're both lying naked on the blanket, I ask several more times if she's sure she wants to continue. The salt of our combined tears mingles with her sweet kisses.

Finally, slowly, I make love to my girl beneath the pale moonlight.

I wonder if I've died and gone to heaven.

———

On the first day of my junior year and Max's sophomore year, I enter the school with her hand firmly grasped inside mine. When the first set of classmates stare at us, I feel her trembling. "This is a bad idea, Noah."

"Everyone's gonna be curious," I say, giving her hand a reassuring squeeze. "You're the first real girl-friend I've had. Let them stare all they want."

She begins to pull away. "But—"

I reel her in close for a quick kiss. She gives in a little, relaxing in my arms. "You're my girl," I whisper into her ear. "Nothing else matters."

"The hell is this?" Travis asks, nudging his way in beside us. His lips tilt with a smirk. "Is she the reason you blew me off all summer? What happened to bros before hoes?"

I release Max to grab Travis by the throat and throw him up against the nearest wall. "Don't you *ever* call her that again! You hear me?"

"Dude, it's just an expression!" he whines, holding his hands out at his sides. "I wasn't calling *her* anything!"

Aware I have the attention of the entire hallway full of students, I quickly release him to reclaim Max's hand. "Max is my girl," I announce in a loud voice. "Anyone who disrespects her is gonna have to answer to me."

Max is quiet as I lead her to her past the juniors to the sophomore hallway. As we pass Tara Harrison, she throws me a dark, dangerous look.

———

Following football practice that early evening, as the team is returning to the bus and the field is only lit by the stadium lights, I catch a shadow stirring beneath the bleachers.

It's Max.

I slap Travis's shoulder pad. "I'll catch up with you later."

"Say hi to your *girl* from me," he answers smartly.

Letting the snarky comment roll off my shoulders, I jog over to Max. When I get closer, I realize she's upset. Fear jolts through me. What if she's here to tell me she's being sent back to her mom's?

"What's wrong?" I ask, my voice urgent. "Did something happen?"

"I can't stop thinking about this morning," she tells me. "You know, with your friend and everything."

"He's an idiot," I say, rubbing her arms. It's freezing cold and she's only wearing one of my flannel shirts over a T-shirt and dress. "It was nothing."

"It's not that...it's just...I don't want you to feel like you always have to defend me. You could've just laughed it off, and no one would've thought anything more about us being together. But now..."

"I'm sorry, Max. I didn't mean to draw attention to you." When I catch the shine of tears in her eyes, I drop a kiss on the top of her head and rub her back. "Hey...why are you crying? Did someone say something to you after that?"

"I don't think you and I—"

"Don't say it," I interrupt, my voice cracking. "You can't break up with me."

"Why *can't* I?" she challenges, stepping back.

"That's not what I meant," I grumble, combing a hand through my hair. "Look, I know something's going on with you that you don't want to talk to me about," I say, stepping closer to gather her chilled hands inside mine. "I've been doing some research at the library, and I think there might be something a doctor could prescribe—something that would help."

Her hands slip from mine. "Help what?"

"With your moody…um…irritability or whatever. It's nothing to be embarrassed about, Max. Especially after everything you've been through."

The dark glare she throws me cuts through my center. "What exactly do you think is wrong with me?"

I glance down, kicking a rock with my cleat. "I just think you might be…um…having some things going on in your head."

"You mean she's a psycho!" a voice cuts through the darkness. Tara Harrison steps into the light behind the field house. Arms folded, she flashes a triumphant smile. "I can't believe you blew me off to go out with a total head-case!"

Max's mouth drops open with a quiet gasp.

"Get the hell outta here, Tara," I warn in a growl. "This conversation has nothing to do with you."

Max turns to run. I sprint after her, calling her name.

Tara releases a wicked laugh into the cold air behind us. "Just wait until everyone hears you're dating a certified psycho! They're gonna eat you both alive!"

"Max, don't listen to her!" I plead when I'm close enough to touch her. "Let's talk about this!"

She stops so suddenly that I'm forced to jump aside to avoid running her over.

"Leave me alone, Noah!" she cries, spinning around. My heart breaks in two from the pain reflected in her eyes and the rush of tears streaking down her face. "I don't ever want to see you again!"

———

Early the next morning, I stop by Max's grandmother's place. I gave Max the night to cool down. I'm hoping she'll talk to me before school starts.

The little old woman beams happily when she sees me. She was probably once beautiful like her granddaughters because she has the same sharp cheekbones and Britta's blue eyes. She once told me she's "extra wrinkly" because she didn't believe in suntan lotion, and it's probably the reason she developed melanoma cancer, too. Since she lost most of her hair from chemo, she usually has a bright scarf around her head. Today, her red scarf matches the polyester pantsuit she's wearing. I bend to give her a careful hug. She's lost weight since her treatments started and can't weigh more than 100 pounds.

"Good morning, Noah!" she greets me, patting my back. "What a nice surprise! I miss seeing you now that you're back in school!"

I draw back with a smile. "Good morning, Becky. Is Max up yet?"

"She called last night and said she was staying with your sister," she says, scratching a gnarled finger over the scarf. "She wanted to help her with a difficult homework assignment." Confusion fills her gaze. "Isn't she there?"

The ground drops out from beneath my feet.

Somehow, I already know.

She's gone back to her mother's in Georgia.

CHAPTER 22
PRESENT DAY

Detective Josephine Kelly

Sitting across from Sheriff Jaros inside his office, I recount what I know about Gabby Gallo and her two dead husbands. While both of their deaths were deemed suspicious, the detectives in charge of each case ruled out any participation by Gabby. They sounded exceptionally unamused when I spoke with them. One of them went so far as to suggest suspecting Gabby Gallo of foul play was a waste of my time.

"I think there's something to be said about her track record," I tell the sheriff. "I get the feeling Gabby Gallo may either have been involved with

Noah Huisman, and she became jealous of his two most recent affairs, or she's protecting her friend, Maxine Huisman, by taking out any threats to the Huismans' marriage. Everything she said when I interviewed her felt well-rehearsed—especially her reaction to Linda Boese's death. I'm sure of it."

"From what I've heard, that Gallo woman is pretty out there and tends to overreact to the smallest things." He runs both hands over his long, lean face. "Besides, that seems like a far stretch of the imagination. Not only that, but those men died in a completely different manner than our two victims. It doesn't track well."

"I agree, but hear me out. In all my years as a homicide detective, I've only been wrong on one occasion, and that's because the killer we arrested had a silent partner. I obviously can't make an arrest based on a feeling, but I hope to obtain a warrant for Ms. Gallo's cellphone records. If I can somehow track her activity around the time of the women's deaths, I'm confident I can prove she was involved."

"What did those detectives in California have to say when you brought them up to speed?"

"One of them said they'd take a second look at the file and get back to me. The other laughed and said if Ms. Gallo had killed her second husband, the mafia would've figured it out by now, and she would've disappeared."

Sheriff Jaros sniffs, then wipes at his nose with the back of his arm. "I'm starting to think what you said the other day might be true. Noah Huisman might be good for both murders."

"I'm not as sure anymore. He returned my call this morning, said he's returning home tonight and would be more than happy to meet with me in the morning. He must've caught on to the fact that he's a potential suspect because he also provided me with a long list of witnesses that can place him out of town on the nights in which both murders took place."

"A man with his kind of money can afford to buy a whole army of witnesses."

"True, but they're worth looking into. It will help if we can verify them and cross him off our list of perps."

He leans back, crossing his legs and resting the heels of his combat boots on the edge of his bulky metal desk. "Do we have any other viable suspects at this point?"

"Not until the B.C.A. submits their report on Britta Baxter's body," I admit. "Your M.E. called yesterday to tell me they finally had a chance to examine her."

"Hopefully, they'll provide us with something

helpful to make a break in both cases. The locals are getting nervous. Word's out we have a serial killer on the loose, looking for a third victim."

I throw him an uneasy look. "At this point, I'm not convinced they're wrong."

When the receptionist announces the sheriff has a phone call from the city administrator, I excuse myself from the room.

For the remainder of the afternoon, I camp out on an empty desk in the rear of the building and reach out to the list of contacts provided by Mr. Huisman. All but one, a restaurant in Manhattan, answer my call. I leave my contact information on a voicemail for the restaurant's manager.

So far, Noah's alibis for the two nights check out. It seems he was in Manhattan the night Britta Baxter was murdered and in St. Paul the night of Linda Boese's. His witnesses include a bevy of credible witnesses, including his company's owner—a man I recognize from a past cover of *Forbes* magazine.

Two hours later, as I power down my laptop and prepare to head back to my rental, I receive a call from the B.C.A. As the officer explains their official findings on Britta Baxter, my phone pings with an email from the restaurant manager.

The large file attached to the email changes everything.

It's dark when I leave the sheriff's office and head to the twin restaurants on the north side of Britta Baxter's bay. At this point, I have enough evidence to rule out both Noah Huisman and Oliver Baxter as suspects. Though I'm not quite having to start from scratch, the investigations have only become more complicated.

With any luck, one of the employees will remember seeing Linda with a man in the past couple of months.

My plan to interview staff changes when I notice the red compact car with an "Aussie mom" sticker on the back window parked directly in front of Key Largo. The sole Tesla known to be in the community is the only other car parked beside it.

Both Molly Boese and Noah Huisman are inside. From the proximity of their cars, I suspect it's no accident.

What in the fresh hell is that about? At least I'll no longer have to wonder if he knew Linda if, in fact, he is here with her sister. But why would they be meeting?

"Just when I was sure he could be cleared as a suspect," I grumble.

I find an open spot in the lot behind them and head inside.

The restaurant side of the establishment is packed with rowdy college kids home on summer break. The twang of country music blares from the digital jukebox as I elbow through the crowd. The thirty-something bartender behind the boat-shaped bar throws me a friendly smile and waves as I approach. "Hey, Detective!"

Wedging myself between two leering men, I return her smile. "Christa, right?"

"The one and only." The woman winks playfully. "What can I get you? A diet soda?"

"You can add a splash of whiskey this time. I'm off duty for the night."

Christa grins as she reaches for an empty glass beneath the bar top. "I'm on it!"

While Christa prepares my drink, I carefully survey my surroundings. It's impossible to see beyond the mass of customers milling about in the immediate section. A pass through the second section and out to the bustling backyard will be necessary to do a thorough job.

"Have you seen Noah Huisman tonight?" I ask Christa.

She shrugs as she gives my drink the last squirt of soda. "No, but this place has been a total zoo since I clocked in at three. Apparently, there's a five-year-class reunion *and* a twenty-first birthday party."

Just my luck.

Christa drops a straw into the drink. "I've been too busy to notice everyone who enters. Plus, sometimes customers come in through the back door by the tiki bar." With a frown, she places the drink in front of me. "If you're thinking of ordering food, I should warn you the kitchen is backed up by at least an hour and a half."

Although my stomach rumbles with the thought of food, I shake my head while tossing a $10 bill out. "I just stopped for a drink."

"Hold on, I'll get your change."

"Keep it," I tell her, already shuffling away.

"Thank you!" Christa calls over the ruckus.

Zig-zagging through the packed crowd, I long to reach for my weapons every time I'm either "accidentally" bumped into by a man or hear a lewd comment directed my way.

Multiple times, I spot a blonde who resembles Molly Boese and a dark-haired man with the potential to be Noah Huisman. The building is so chaotic that I can hardly blame myself for desperately wanting to locate them.

My phone buzzes with an incoming call from the holster on my hip. I retrieve it to find a 408 number.

California. Locating a quieter corner, I push against one ear to block the excessive noise before answering. "Detective Kelly."

"It's Detective Wendorf," a gruff voice answers in a hint of an accent straight out of the Bronx. I picture a heavy-set man with a thick mustache and a stain from lunch on his obnoxious tie. "I'm calling back in regards to Gabby Gallo."

"Did you find something suspicious?"

Detective Wendorf lets out a slow, noisy breath. "You could say that."

CHAPTER 23
PRESENT DAY

Beth

Concealed in a dark corner of the tiki bar behind Key Largo, I watch with disdain as the nosy detective exits back through the restaurant's front door. *Good riddance.* God knows what she thought she'd discover by comin' here tonight.

The live band playin' hillbilly music on a semi-trailer overlookin' the water has provided enough of a distraction that no one has paid me any attention. I swing my gaze back to the first table right inside the doors where the dead bartender's twin and Noah sit across from each other. Although I'd missed their initial meetin', Noah appeared twitchy enough by the time I arrived that I was certain she was makin' him uncomfortable.

By the time his glass of amber liquid becomes empty, he's swayin' and occasionally closin' his eyes. He's on the verge of passin' out at the table. Molly takes his arm and guides him through the door leadin' outside in my direction.

The feral side of me wants to scream. Molly's too young and too damn pretty, just like her bitch of a sister.

I don't know what Gabby and Maxine could've possibly been thinkin' when they brought her into their plan, but they're idiots.

I, for one, don't trust her or her intentions.

Who's to say she won't call the police? She could ruin my plan to make Noah pay for his infidelities.

What's stoppin' this girl from becomin' Noah's next affair?

I hustle around the end of tiki bar shaped like a boat and nestle in on Noah's other side. "Easy, big fella," I coo, wedgin' my shoulder under his armpit and wrappin' my arm around his thick waist. "I got you."

Givin' me a double-take, Molly flinches. "What are *you* doing here?" Her eyes flicker over my hair.

"You're still recognizable, you know. And this wasn't part of the plan."

"It's okay," I answer through gritted teeth. "I'll take over from here."

Noah's unfocused gaze lands on me before his mouth tilts with a smolderin' grin. "Hey, sexy."

"Hey there, darlin'," I reply. "Miss me?"

He nudges his nose against my cheek. "Always, baby."

"You can *leave now*, Molly," I say, ensurin' my voice is firm enough to convey a threat. "I brought his boat over. We'll be fine without on our own."

Wisely, Molly releases her hold on Noah. "But—"

"Do *not* make me repeat myself," I seethe with a final warnin' glare aimed in her direction. "Everythin' will still work out. I'll fill you in on the details in the mornin'."

Wisely, she doesn't attempt to stop me.

———

Noah groans in a non-sexual way. It still stirs up the dark desires I feel whenever he's around—especially since I've secured him to a chair and have the freedom to do whatever I want. The way the deep shadows from the construction lightbulbs illuminate his handsome face and full lips makes it harder to keep my hands to myself.

His heavy lids lift slightly. "Where'm I?" he slurs. "What's goin' on?"

"Shhh, don't hurt yourself, darlin'." I lodge my foot on the chair between his legs and brandish the bonin' knife I'd grabbed from the kitchen, holdin' it near his throat. "This will all be over soon."

"*Beth?*" He blinks rapidly until his pupils come into focus. All at once, he sits a little taller, seemingly more alert, and cautiously eyes the knife. "What're you doin'? What's this? Why're we in the basement?"

"You're goin' down for Britta and Linda's murders. It's time for you to pay the price for bein' an unfaithful bastard."

"*Unfaithful?* Are you insane?" With a cold, harsh bark of a laugh, he twists around, testin' the rope's strength. "I don't care what kind of sick game you're playing this time, Beth. I'm done. I refuse to play anymore. I wanna talk to Max."

"Maxine is too vulnerable around you—just like she was with her cousin. She actually believes you're a good man. She was somehow convinced Britta was good to her, too. She obviously needed my protection from both of you."

"*I want to talk to Max,*" he repeats, his face stony.

"You don't deserve to talk to your wife!" I roar.

"She's too innocent—too *wholesome* for a deceitful son-of-a-bitch like you!"

Eyes closed, he gives a slight shake of his head. "What did I do this time?"

"Do you seriously need me to spell it out for you? First, you impregnated her cousin—"

The hateful look he casts makes me grateful he's incapacitated. "Max is well aware of everything that happened between Britta and me!"

"Does she know you're still sleepin' with her?"

"'*Still*'? Don't be ridiculous! It's been *twenty-two* years since I've been with Britta!" Spittle flies from his lips with every 't.' "She wanted to pick up where we left off when she moved here, but I told her it was over! I love Max! I'd never let another woman come between us!"

I let his "confession" soak in. Either he's tellin' the truth, or he's become delusional enough to believe what he's sayin' is true. Is it possible I misread the situation between them? There's no way I'm wrong about them. Is there? "What about that bartender?"

"Like I told her sister, I *never* slept with Linda." His eyes flicker to the stairway. "Hold on. What happened to Molly? I only agreed to meet with her because she said she had concerns about my wife. Next thing I knew—"

"Why did you have a picture of Linda's tits on

your phone?" I demand, pressin' the knife's edge against his Adam's apple.

"How the—" He lets out a roar of fury. "Damn it, Beth, I'm done talking to you! You're out of control!"

I push the knife a little harder, piercin' his skin. Seein' blood against the blade makes my heart pump a little faster. I'll do whatever it takes to protect Maxine, even if it means eliminatin' the love of her life.

"Why did Linda send you that picture?" I yell.

"She didn't! Oliver sent it to me at Britta's visitation!" he shouts back, his voice boomin' through the concrete space. With a shake of his head, he regains control of his rage. "That prick wanted to prove that he didn't give a damn about what happened between me and his wife. He told me he was leaving the service early to bang some local girl he'd been seeing. He's had it out for me since he learned the truth about Taylor."

Doubt niggles at my mind. Eyein' him skeptically, I loosen my grip on the knife. "You're becomin' a brilliant liar, Noah."

"It's the fucking truth!" Any hint of color drains from his face as his spine becomes ramrod straight. "Wait a minute. Is that why you killed Britta and Linda? Because you thought I was cheating on Max?"

Jilted laughter spills from my lips. "What makes you think I killed them?"

"I found the knife you used, Beth. The one you stole from Britta's kitchen. I know it was you. There's no way Max would've hurt her cousin. I stashed it down here to protect you…*and* Max. I worried Detective Kelly would eventually catch on to what happened. I planned to hide it until the heat was off us, and it was safe to discard it elsewhere."

Memories from the night Britta left this world return in a disjointed haze that takes my breath away.

She struggles for air as water fills her lungs, wavin' her hands around her head, desperately kickin' her legs before the light leaves her eyes, and she dies a slow, torturous death.

That night was supposed to remain my little secret.

Guess I wasn't as careful as I thought.

I hold Noah's stare momentarily before givin' a slow, sarcastic clap. "Well done, Noah. It's like you said—all those years of watchin' true crime with Kathy must've made you a murder expert."

"I hadn't been with Britta since she got pregnant with Taylor, dammit! And I never hooked up with that bartender! You're delusional, Beth! I realize it's your job to protect Max, but you know damn well

I'm fully aware of everything she went through! I would never do anything to make her distrust me—not in a million years!"

The door upstairs creaks open. Noah throws me a wide-eyed look as heavy footsteps descend on the stairway, but he's too intelligent to yell for help. He'd be puttin' Maxine in danger.

Gabby comes into view, awkwardly grippin' a small pistol in both hands with the finesse of a small child. "What's going on down here?" she demands, her narrowed gaze jumpin' back and forth between Noah and me. "Where's Molly? What'd you do with her? This wasn't part of the plan."

"You shouldn't have trusted her with him," I scold, gesturin' to Noah. "It was like danglin' a piece of meat in front of a lion."

"Gabby, put the gun down," Noah pleads, twistin' to loosen the rope. "I'm sure Beth has been filling you in with her demented version of things, but Max must've told you how I've tried my best to protect her. I didn't sleep with either Britta or Linda!"

Gabby's eyes roll in his direction. "Oh, so Taylor came about via immaculate conception?"

"That's the last time I slept with her! I care about Max more than anything in this world! I would never hurt her that way! I regret ever engaging in conversation with Britta! I only hung out with her at first because she reminded me of Max!"

A haze fills my peripheral vision.

I'm about to lose control.

Not now, dammit.

"He's tellin' the truth about one thing," I tell Gabby with a mournful shake of my head. "He actually does care about us. He's been tryin' to help us for years."

Gabby lowers the gun and purses her lips. "Wait a minute. I'm confused. When you say 'us,' do you mean you and Max? You're talking about the two of you collectively? I thought Beth was the one who wore the wig and bright lipstick. Was I wrong?"

"No, Gabby. You're exactly right." I remove the wig from my head and drop it onto the concrete floor. "But Maxine is about to take over."

CHAPTER 24
23 MONTHS EARLIER

Noah

It's after midnight when I park my Tesla inside the garage. My flight from New York was delayed by several hours, but Max promised she'd wait up for me. Although our rekindled relationship hasn't progressed beyond heated kisses and wandering touches, I'm okay with it. It's a reminder that she's still the same fragile girl I met as a teenager. Even though she claimed to be okay the one time I tried pushing the subject, her actions would suggest otherwise.

I toe my loafers off inside the door and shuffle

through the dark house, tossing my overnight bag next to the unmade bed before heading into the master bathroom. Max must've been here and left since I made the bed before leaving town. Sometimes, I worry one of these days, she will disappear again, just like when we were kids.

When I flip on the set of lights over the vanity mirror, I see a reflection of Max leaning against the doorway of my walk-in closet behind me.

My shout of surprise sticks inside my throat. She wears the hottest lace lingerie I've ever laid eyes on. The black material looks painted on her skin the way it accentuates the heavy swells of her breasts. She's also donning a straight blond wig and bright red lipstick. I never would have imagined Max owned anything so risqué. It's somehow both enduring and disturbing at the same time.

Something isn't right.

"Max, *sweetheart*, you almost gave me a heart attack."

"My name's Beth," she purrs in a deep, seductive voice.

"Beth?" I repeat, lifting my eyebrows.

"That's right." Slipping in behind me, she grinds against my backside. "Won't be long before you'll associate my name with pleasure." She kisses my neck before clamping her teeth over a section of skin. Meanwhile, her hands work on releasing my trousers.

With a quiet growl, I close my eyes. On some level, I realize something's amiss. I should stop her from going any further. But my body can't resist her seductive touch. "We should talk about this. If you're not ready—"

"Oh, I'm ready, darlin'." As soon as my trousers fall around my feet, she tugs on the band of my boxers. "I've been ready to do this for *years*."

Unable to fight against the heat coiling inside me, I reel around to capture her mouth with mine. She responds in kind with a lustful rush of vigor that almost knocks me on my ass. It's hot as hell. It's also too aggressive.

It isn't like her.

I draw back and take her face in my hands. Words can't express what it means to witness the beautiful girl I cared so much about becoming a strong, confident woman with more sex appeal than I know what to do with. Yet her smile's off. There's also something different about the spark set deep in her eyes.

"I've been fantasizing about making love to you again for weeks, sweetheart. Hell, *decades*. But we should slow it down a little...take our time." Emotion burns behind my eyes when I slide my thumbs along her slim jawline. "I still love you, Maxine. I never stopped."

Her lips harden with a feral scowl. *"My name is Beth!"* She rises on her toes and catches my earlobe with her teeth, biting hard enough to leave an impression of her teeth.

I almost choke on my tongue. "What the—"

"Don't you remember me, handsome?" She drags her nose along my jaw. "We've met before...back when you were a horny teenager too afraid to make a move on sweet Maxine."

Rocked with the memory of how she suddenly became aggressive the first time I confessed my love for her, I suck in a shallow breath. She became randomly sexual, almost identical to how she's acting now. *An internal switch flipped.* "Are you into role-playing, or is this something else?"

With a throaty sigh, she shoves herself away from me. "Men can be so daft." She yanks on a vanity drawer and retrieves a pack of cigarettes from the far back.

I watch in awe as she removes a small lighter from the inside and lights a smoke between her red lips. I'm too shocked to ask how the cigarettes ended up in my bathroom drawer or tell her I don't allow anyone to smoke in my home.

"You obviously don't get it," she says before

taking a long drag. Smoke billows from her nose as she throws me a pointed look. "Maxine is far too messed up to have kinky sex with a man. Her momma's piece of shit boyfriend made sure of that. I'm here to get the job done. I have to protect her from all the things she can't handle."

The truth hits me with the impact of a sucker punch to the face. I've sensed something more profound has been going on with her since we first met. I was convinced her mood swings were because she had undiagnosed bipolar disorder. But this goes far beyond a simple change in mood. The lipstick and wig are part of a different persona, just like the drastic change of clothes she donned as a kid.

Another forgotten memory returns, this one from an old mini-series I once watched from my mom's extensive VCR collection. The main character, played by Sally Field, experienced blackouts, and a psychiatrist diagnosed her as having several different personalities as a direct result of her mother's abuse. Is that what this is?

The notion that Max may be dealing with something so complex and dark rockets a harsh jolt through my bones. How did I not see the signs earlier?

She's watching me closely as I process everything. "You have multiple personalities."

Her lush, red lips spread with a satisfied smile. "Ladies and gentlemen, give the man a prize!" Laughing manically, she taps the cigarette ashes into my marble sink. "You got it, although that term's outdated. They call it dissociative identity disorder now."

Lips pursed, she studies my expression. "I'm surprised you don't look at least a *little* freaked out by this information. Maxine's first husband hit the road once he realized the truth. Well, other factors were involved. She also didn't want to bring children into a world that allowed innocent little girls to be habitually abused by predators. The fact that she was secretly takin' birth control became the final straw that broke that moron's back."

The room spins as I watch the virtual stranger before me take another drag of the cigarette. How did I not understand the complexities of her situation back in high school? It dawns on me that she's using a Southern dialect stronger than the occasional soft drawls she sometimes slips into.

"How many personalities are there?"

"Far as I can tell, it's only been me and Maxine for a while now. I kept Roger in line after he became a little aggressive, but I haven't been around much since. At least not until the day you came back into her life. There were a few others—one being a sweet little thing afraid of her own shadow, but the weaker ones tend to die off once I take charge. I don't have time for whiney babies, and I won't let anyone else take the light whenever Maxine needs me."

Unease tightens my chest. "Beth" is letting me know she won't be pushed around or mistreated. "Can Max hear me right now?"

"Not likely. She tends to stay in the dark when I take over."

Somehow, speaking to this alter personality feels like a severe betrayal to Max. Worse than the time Britta spilled Max's secret all those years ago. Still, as long as she's willing to talk to me this way, I hope to glean the information Max refused to share. "Where did you—*Max*—go that fall of my junior year? Why did she run away?"

"Because you *humiliated her*, you imbecile!" The way her expression hardens, I believe everything she's saying about this disorder. There's no sign of Max when she screams, "*You made her think she was broken!*"

I start to reach for her, wanting to provide comfort, but the sharpness in her glare makes me think better of it. "It wasn't my intention to embarrass her! If I'd known Tara was spying on us, I never would've said those things! Can you please just tell me where she went?" I fist both hands inside my hair and lean back on the vanity. "Don't tell me she returned to her mom's. I don't think I could live with that."

"She returned to Georgia alright, but I made damn sure she'd never have to deal with that pedophile, *Martin*, ever again."

"What do you mean?" I study her face, wondering if she's implying precisely what I'm assuming. Is she capable of murder? "How'd you do that?"

With a teasing smile, she sucks in more nicotine. "Don't you worry your sexy head over it, darlin'. I told you it's my job to protect her, and I got the job done."

My mind races with the possibilities. "Have you...I mean...is Max seeing anyone? Like a doctor or a therapist?"

Humor sparks her eyes. "Why, so they can tell her she's crazy?"

"So they can try to help her. Both of you."

She looks away, shrugging. "When the state stepped in and took her away from her momma, the judge made her see a psychiatrist. That's when they diagnosed her with D.I.D. At first, Maxine was relieved. It explained all the lapses in time. Then she realized no one would want anythin' to do with her if they knew the truth, so I've done my best to help her keep it hidden. Her psychotic momma extorted thousands from us after she learned about Maxine's condition."

Momentarily gripping the sides of my head, I wince. "Hold on. Max said she used her savings to pay for her mom's *rehab*."

"Maxine lied. She didn't think you'd wanna be with her anymore if you knew about us."

Strong emotion stings my eyes. This is partially my fault. If I had spoken up when we were kids, she wouldn't have spent *decades* battling this dark secret alone.

"I still want her in my life," I insist, my voice gruff. "Maybe even more than before. I could go to a therapist along with her. They could help me understand the complexities of this diagnosis a little better."

Smashing the cigarette's cherry against the sink, she tosses it aside before tugging on my shirt to draw me closer. "We're perfectly happy with the way things are, especially now that she brought your sexy ass back into our lives."

When she resumes kissing my neck, I shake my head. It's the most confusing situation I've ever found myself in. The woman I love may not be aware of what's happening.

"This doesn't feel right," I say, giving her a gentle

nudge. "It's like we're sneaking around behind Max's back."

"Beth" glides her fingers through my hair, her velvety lips twisting with a wicked grin. "Trust me when I say Maxine wants this. She's always wanted this with you, like that night you made love to her at the park under the stars. She's just too messed up to go after it again."

Guilt for not doing anything to help her, for not asking my mom to intervene, weighs heavy on my conscience. I yank her against me for a searing kiss. Whatever's going on inside her brain doesn't change the fact that I love the woman standing in front of me. I'll do everything in my power to help her now that I know the truth.

———

After making several calls and watching a dozen informative videos the following morning, I run to Sioux Falls while Max spends the day with Britta. She seemed a little confused when she woke nestled inside my arms. Thankfully, her other persona, Beth, insisted on wearing one of my dress shirts to bed so Max wouldn't panic when she "took over the light," as Beth calls it.

Max kissed me before she left and stated she was

glad we'd finally made love. I could sense in her hesitant tone that she only made an assumption. It was disappointing that she seemingly wasn't present when I'd told her how much I loved her as she climaxed beneath me. And Beth's assertive nature erased any hope of the tenderness I'd been looking forward to.

By the time I return home early evening, my mind's still reeling over everything I learned about Max and her "alter" personality. Every article I could find online suggested dissociative identity (or "D.I.D." as it's commonly called) is typically triggered by a childhood trauma. The instinct to lock all the doors and spend the rest of my life protecting Max from any more harm is suffocating. I needed to do something drastic.

When I spot her car pulling into the driveway a couple hours later, I kill the lights and cue the selected playlist so Kurt Cobain is singing "And I Love Her" when she steps through the front door.

Illuminated by the dozens of candles I'd lit around the room, her eyes widen at the velvet box in my hand. "Noah—"

"What's going on?" Britta demands, appearing on the threshold behind Max. She regards the diamond ring like it's a bomb about to detonate. "What in the *hell* do you think you're doing?"

Eyes closed, I give her a slight shake of my head. "This has nothing to do with you, Britta."

"The hell it doesn't!" She nudges Max aside and holds a hand up between us. "You don't know her as well as you think, Noah. She's going through a lot of shit! You can't make someone this fragile…this *broken*…your wife!"

As I step forward, I have to remind myself I would never hit a woman. "Get out of my goddamn house before I throw you out!"

She releases a hard laugh. "You can't—"

Max swings her fist, throwing a solid punch against Britta's jaw and sending her down to the floor. "Shut the hell up, Britta! He's right! This has *nothin'* to do with you! Stop tryin' to control everyone else and worry about your own disaster of a life for a change!"

"I can't believe you hit me!" Britta pouts, cradling her jaw while scrambling to her feet. She wags a finger at me. "See what you'll have to put up with? She's crazy! One minute, she acts sweet and innocent, then she turns on you and becomes this insanely angry person with a redneck accent!"

"*Goodbye*, Britta," I seethe through a clenched jaw.

As Britta stomps back outside, part of me wants to high-five Max for standing up to her overbearing cousin. Then I remember—everything has changed.

Max wasn't the one who threw the punch. Now that I know to listen to the pronunciation of her vowels and the way she drops her 'g's, it's a dead giveaway.

Once again, I'm standing face-to-face with Beth.

CHAPTER 25
PRESENT DAY

Maxine

Darkness dissipates around the edges of my vision as I return to the light. It takes me a moment to catch my breath and find my bearings.

I'm in the basement of our house, with Gabby and Noah.

She's holding a gun.

He's tied to a chair.

Blood trickles from his neck.

There's something metal clenched in my hand.

I look down to see a knife from our kitchen.

I drop it, flinching when it clatters against the concrete.

Beth was here.

"Oh, god!" I cry, rushing to my husband's side. Fortunately, the cut on his neck doesn't appear to be deep enough for stitches. I begin loosening the rope. "What did she do to you? Are you okay?"

"It's just a nick," he assures me in a comforting tone. "I'm okay."

Gabby carelessly waves the gun through the air. "*Maxine*, you seem to be forgetting the reason we're in this situation to begin with. Molly called me as soon as your badass side hijacked your husband. She said she was just getting to the good part."

"This has gone too far," I say, releasing the last knot. "Beth can't be trusted. She could've killed him."

Noah springs from the chair and pulls me into his arms. "She was only trying to protect you," he says, stopping to press a long kiss against my temple. "She was convinced I was cheating on you, but I told her I haven't been with Britta since she learned she was pregnant, and I had nothing to do with Linda. I think Beth finally realized I was telling the truth."

Huffing, Gabby shakes her head. "I'm starting to understand why you two are perfect for each other. You're both nuts." She aims the gun at Noah. "You may have conned that Beth chick into believing you, but I still think you did it. I think you killed Brit and Linda."

My belly twists in half when it dawns on me that she could be right. We still don't know who killed them. But if Noah had nothing to do with either of the women, who else would've wanted them dead?

You know damn well who, a voice scolds.

Taking a step closer to Noah, Gabby gives him a smug smile. "I have firsthand knowledge of how easy it is to get away with murder. Do you truly believe it was a mere coincidence that *both* of my wealthy husbands passed away, making me one of the richest bitches alive? I had the freaking *mob* after me for a hot minute, but I was able to convince them of my innocence."

"Wait—you *seriously* killed your husbands?" I ask, unable to mask my shock. "Gabby…"

"Goes to show how easy it is to manipulate someone into thinking you're innocent," she replies. "Don't think for a minute Romeo over here isn't capable of doing the same." She gestures his way with the gun. "You can stand there with your smoldering looks and profess your innocence to your hot, completely cuckoo wife all you want, but I'm not buying it."

A ruckus comes from upstairs. The door at the top

of the stairway swings open, and a flurry of uniformed officers storm down the steps. Sheriff Jaros and Detective Kelly take the lead, both wearing Kevlar jackets.

"Drop your weapon and get down on your knees!" Detective Kelly commands, aiming her gun at Gabby. She reaches the bottom step and slowly creeps in closer. "Don't make me shoot you, Gabby! We can get you the help you need!"

"Help?" Gabby shouts over her shoulder, waving the gun in our direction. "The only thing I need help with is putting this man behind bars! He slept with those poor women and killed them so they couldn't blab about it to his wife!"

"That's not true!" Noah insists, stepping around me as a shield against the threat of impending gunfire.

Detective Kelly shuffles in a little more. "Put the gun down, Gabby, and we'll discuss the situation like civilized adults."

"I'm not the one you should be worried about," Gabby pouts. "Why aren't you arresting him?"

"Because we recently received video footage from a restaurant in New York. He was meeting with clients at a hotel bar in Chelsea the night Britta was murdered. The camera captured a crystal-clear image that leaves no question of his identity. A waitress also confirmed he was there. She remembered her interaction with him because of the sizable tip he left. He couldn't have killed Britta."

"Well…I…but…but…" Gabby stammers, glancing between Noah and me. Her arm relaxes, recklessly lowering the gun. "Then who did?"

Detective Kelly pounces on Gabby, disarming her and pinning her face down on the concrete floor in one fluid move. "Gabby Gallo, you're under arrest for the murders of John Williams and Paul Gallo. Anything you say—"

"Now, wait a minute!" Gabby pleads from beneath her, not bothering to fight as her hands are cuffed behind her back. "I was cleared for those *years* ago!"

"New evidence came to light," the detective tells her. "We'll go through everything once you're booked at the station." She continues to recite Gabby's rights.

"I want my lawyer!" Gabby cries as two of the deputies help her back onto her feet. "Give me a phone so I can call my lawyer! When this is over, she'll have every last one of your badges!"

While everyone else in the room is tending to Gabby, Noah swipes the knife from our kitchen off the floor and slips it into his back jeans pocket.

"Go ahead and take her in," Detective Kelly tells the sheriff. "I'll be right behind you."

"I want my lawyer! I want my lawyer! I want my lawyer!" Gabby chants like a child throwing a tantrum as they lead her up the stairway.

Detective Kelly turns to us and briefly studies Noah's neck. "What happened there?"

"It got nicked in a scuffle with Gabby when she tied me to the chair," he lies, dabbing at it with his fingertips. He then wraps me beneath his arm in a firm grip. "We're just grateful you got here when you did, Detective."

Her gaze sweeps through the basement, pausing on the chair and rope. "I'm going to need you both to come to the Sheriff's Station in Slayton to piece together what happened here tonight."

"Can it wait until morning?" Noah asks. "It's been a long day."

"I suppose that would be alright," she decides. Her gaze flips back and forth between us. "Just so you know, the B.C.A. determined it was most likely a woman who stabbed Britta. Not only that, the county's medical examiner found traces of benzodiazepines in Linda Boese's system. It's the same drug Gabby's second husband allegedly overdosed on."

A crippling cold washes over my bones.

Gabby had given me several benzos when I couldn't sleep.

Detective Kelly's observant gaze rolls onto me. "I don't imagine it will be long until we can charge Gabby with both your cousin's death and Linda's."

"Thanks again for your help, Detective," Noah tells her with a somewhat dismissive nod. "We'll come to the station right away in the morning."

Detective Kelly gives me a thoughtful look like she's about to say something more. After a beat, she nods and follows the deputies up the stairway.

With a heavy sigh, Noah pulls me into his arms for a suffocating hug. "We can finally put this nightmare behind us."

"Gabby didn't kill Brit and Linda," I whisper against his shoulder.

"It's late." He draws back with a loving smile, lacing his fingers around mine. "Let's go to bed. We'll discuss everything in the morning."

Refusing to give in when he tugs my hand, I firmly plant my feet. "I found Britta's knife down here, stashed in the ceiling. At first, I thought maybe you did it, but it was her. *Beth*. Like you said, she was trying to protect me."

His gaze drifts down to the floor. "Max—"

Gasping, I yank my hand out from his and stumble back. "You knew, didn't you? You hid the knife Beth used to cut you and lied about Gabby scratching you because you were afraid the detective would catch on to the truth." I squeeze my hands into fists at my sides. "I can't let Gabby go down for something I did."

"The hell you can't!" Fire lights his eyes when he locks his fingers around my wrists. "It sounds like she's already going away for killing her husbands. You heard her—she confessed to it! She's going to prison anyway!" When I still refuse to budge, he lets out a harsh sigh. "Beth once told me you're unaware of the things she does. I didn't believe her until I found Britta's knife stashed in the bottom of the garbage bin, covered in blood. I was certain she had killed your cousin as much as I was certain you didn't have any involvement in the act. *You* didn't kill them, Max. I refuse to let you take the fall for something *Beth* did! I won't let you rot in some prison cell for this!"

"What's going to stop Beth from killing again? What if she becomes even more paranoid and begins to suspect you're sleeping with every single woman you come into contact with?"

"I'll make damn sure she never hurts anyone again," he declares with a determined look. "I'll quit my job and we'll move to some remote island in another country. I'll hire the best psychiatrist specializing in D.I.D. to treat you. We can do this if we work together, Max. I can keep you safe."

"What if she tries to kill *you*? She held a knife to your neck, Noah. I have no idea of knowing whether she actually intended to kill you, but I can't stand back and trust that she won't do it again." Eyes watering, I wiggle free from his grip to touch his face. "I couldn't live with myself if she hurt you."

His jaw hardens when he shakes his head. "Do you hear yourself? *You don't know her intentions*. That also means you're not responsible for her actions. You shouldn't have to suffer for her lack of control!"

Extreme warmth spreads throughout my body. Since the day Noah stood up for me in the school hallway, I've cherished and adored him more than anyone who has come into my life. Before now, I was too afraid to classify those feelings, to express them with the proper words. Although it's the kind of thing normal, healthy couples in a committed relationship tell each other, I've always associated the three little words with unfathomable darkness and depravity.

Tears spill down my cheeks as I reach up to frame his face with my hands. "I love you, Noah. I'm sorry I've never told you before, even though it's always been true. Those words…he used to say them to me before—"

"You can't leave me again," he interrupts, his voice breaking. "Please, sweetheart. Don't do this. We've already wasted *decades* because I wasn't man enough to help you when you needed me the first time. I'm not going to let you walk away from me again without putting up a fight!"

I silence him with a kiss. I can't expect him to agree with my decision.

I can only hope that by turning myself in, I'll protect him from the monster inside.

And I know she's listening.

The too-familiar feeling that we're being watched slithers down my spine.

CHAPTER 26

THE NIGHT OF BRITTA'S DEATH

Beth

One night while Noah's away on business, I decide it's time to finally reveal myself to Britta. As often as we've met, she's never seen me in my purest form. I apply my favorite shade of scarlet lipstick and wiggle into a corset with snakeskin leggings before headin' out for the girls' night Maxine had marked on her calendar.

A sliver of the moon provides the smallest amount of light as I row across the bay to her monstrosity of a house, glowin' from dozens of lights within. The bitch is on clear display as she makes her way around the minimalist kitchen, precisely as intended when she'd drawn up the house plans.

Britta Baxter thrives beneath the limelight, whether online or in person. Her only wish in life is to be worshipped.

I've never understood how Maxine can tolerate her cousin's behavior.

Once I've tied the boat to the dock, I saunter upstairs to the kitchen. "Hello, *Britta*," I sneer. "Time to teach you a little lesson."

"What are you talking about?" She glances up to eye my blond hair and bursts out laughing. "Oh...my god!" she wheezes, cradlin' her stomach as tears stream down her cheeks. "Max! You look *ridiculous*!"

"My name's not Max," I drawl, stridin' toward her in 4-inch stilettos.

Once her amusement is under control, she begins to pour two glasses of Prosecco while slowly shakin' her head. "I don't know what's up with the wig and accent, but I'm sure Noah would *love* that slutty outfit and the lipstick." Grinnin', she throws me a wink. "Maybe there's a chance you won't die alone after all, Max."

"I'm not Max," I repeat. "Maxine is weak. I'm tired of watchin' her get pushed around by you."

"What are you *talking* about?" she scoffs, setting the bottle down. Her grin turns into a frown. "I'm used to the psycho bit with that accent, but this is a bit extreme."

"The name's Beth."

Her eyes grow wider. "Wait. Are you saying that time I walked into your house and heard Noah having wild sex, he was calling *you* that name?"

"Yes, you twit. Try to keep up."

When I stride next to her and snatch one of the glasses, her eyes scan down my skin-tight leggings.

"So the name's just part of some kinky game between the two of you?"

"It's much more than that," I assure her in a sultry voice. "I first came around when Maxine was a little girl...back when her poor brain couldn't deal with the sick and twisted things her evil mother allowed to happen. I'm here to protect her from any other evil that comes into her life—includin' you."

Her lips curl with a small smile. "So what... you're some kind of schizophrenic? *That's* what's been wrong with you all these years?"

Knowin' the truth is too complex for her tiny brain, I laugh sharply. "You aren't gonna deny you're evil? You're the only relative remainin' in Maxine's life. You could've been there for her, but instead, you chose to create a toxic relationship with her from the beginnin'."

"Toxic?" Her eyes roll to the ceilin'. "Don't be

ridiculous. I care about you, Max. I've always looked out for you, haven't I?"

With a hand on my hip, I shake my head. "Are you going to stand there and pretend you haven't pursued every single man to come into Maxine's life?"

Liftin' her chin, she looks down at me over the bridge of her narrow nose. "It's not my fault they found me more attractive."

"You're so vain, Britta. After all the surgeries and becomin' a social media star, you're *still* worried you're not receivin' the proper attention." Bracin' one arm beneath my breasts, I take a sip of the bubbly drink and smirk. "So you're claimin' Noah *chose* you over Maxine because you were better lookin'?"

"He couldn't keep his hands off of me."

"Was that before or after you drugged him?"

Lips pressed in a white line, she snags the other glass of Prosecco. "Good luck proving that." She chugs it down in one breath before pourin' herself another glass. "Listen, *Max*, or Beth, or whatever the hell name your psycho ass—"

"When Noah refused to be involved with you a second time, you drugged him after you stopped takin' your birth control. You figured he'd *have to* stick around if you became pregnant. And when *that* plan backfired, you went after Maxine's *new* boyfriend and tricked him into thinkin' *he* was the father. You were willin' to do whatever it took to hurt Maxine the most."

Redness seeps into her complexion. *"Oliver* made the first move. He was bored with your crazy ass and was looking for a release. I merely knocked on your apartment door one night. He was all over me the second he answered."

"You knew Maxine was workin' that day. Oliver later told her that you came to their apartment wearin' a raincoat and nothin' else. You made your intentions clear from the start." I set my empty glass down with a snort. "You did Maxine a favor with that one." I pour myself another glass. "Aside from you tryin' to convince Noah to have sex again after Maxine returned, that leaves us with good ol' Rog. I suppose you were especially eager to get your hands on him once you realized Max might *actually* be in love."

"Roger *came to me* after he suspected something was wrong. When you first started acting all moody, he figured you were pregnant. Then he found your birth control pills and realized you'd been lying to him. He was so upset—I thought he was going to break something. I held him until he stopped trembling with rage. One thing led to another…and that's when you walked in."

"Do you hear yourself?" I ask, leanin' in close until our noses almost touch. "You're tryin' to make everythin' you did with those men sound innocent. In reality, you're nothin' more than a sociopath."

"You never deserved a happy ending!" she sneers, spittle flying from her lips. "It's *your fault* my dad left us! I had to grow up without knowing a father's love. If it weren't for you and your whore of a mom—"

"*Your dad* sexually abused an innocent child!" I yell back. "Nothing about him leaving you was Maxine's fault! She was the only real victim in all of this! Your momma and Maxine's momma both knew what was goin' on, and neither of them did a damn thing to stop it!"

When she only appears annoyed by my declaration, blindin' rage zips beneath my skin. I slip a knife from the butcher block on the counter beside me. "I'm sick and tired of you punishin' Maxine for somethin' she had no control over!" My fingers vibrate around the knife when I raise it.

With an expression of terror, Britta raises her hands. "What are you doing? Max, put that down! Stop it! You're scaring me!"

With a deep scowl, I start for her. "I'm gonna make sure you're done ruinin' Maxine's life once and for all."

EPILOGUE

6 Months Later
Detective Josephine Kelly

Silence blankets the Minnesota Security Hospital as I hand my service weapon and badge to a guard. "I haven't been here in a while," I comment. "Can't say I remember it being this quiet."

The stout woman lifts her shoulders, appearing unceremoniously bored by her occupation. "Most of the patients are outside, playing in the snow. The rest are in session with their psychiatrists." She doesn't look away from her computer monitor when she returns the manilla envelope I'd also handed over for inspection. "You're all set."

The woman buzzes me through the locked doors. I start down the long, tiled hallway, dotted with several sets of elemental doorways a mere moment before I spot the person I came to see.

A lithe, curly-haired brunette with a heavy dose of freckles dotting her pale skin stands before me, reviewing a chart clipped to the wall. Having researched Dr. Laura Scanlan extensively, I recognize the woman from various pictures posted online. Dr. Scanlan graduated in the top 2% of her graduating class at Johns Hopkins and has received countless awards throughout her tenure as a respected psychiatrist. She's a renowned advocate for patients with dissociative identity disorder, having presented at numerous mental health symposiums and universities all across the country.

"Dr. Scanlan, I'm Detective Josephine Kelly," I introduce myself, handing her the manilla envelope. "I got you that court order you requested."

The doctor removes the papers from the envelope and gives them a brief glance before flashing me a terse smile. Pale green eyes make the woman appear both intriguing and trustworthy. "Let's have this conversation in my office," she suggests.

I follow her long, precise strides through another

set of security doors, then into a large office at the end of a short hallway. The doctor sits behind a metal desk framed by textbooks with faded and ripped spines. I sit on the opposite side, noting the space is orderly and devoid of any personal decor, which is likely done out of necessity. Patients may wander into the room and use almost anything as a weapon.

"Let me start this with an important question, Detective Kelly." The doctor folds her arms over the desk. "What do you know about dissociative identity disorder?"

"Not a whole lot," I answer truthfully. "I've researched it extensively since Maxine Huisman's last hearing, and I must say I'm still at a loss. It sounds like something a patient could easily emulate to avoid prison time."

"You were there for the court hearings. You heard the testimony. Both Maxine's mother and Noah Huisman stated Maxine had exhibited signs of D.I.D. back when she was a teenager. The extreme mood swings, changes in appearance and dialect, impulsiveness, suspicion, anxiety...they're all classic signs of the disorder. Her mother suspected it may have even started long before then. However, I'm skeptical of everything that woman claimed considering she turned a blind eye to her daughter's abuse. And let's not forget the testimony of the social worker who placed Maxine with her grandmother after the snake-bite incident. It's close to impossible for a child to have planned to emulate those symptoms to be acquitted of murder several decades in the future."

"Regardless of Mrs. Baxter's mental state, she was still present when she committed the murders. Am I right?"

"Physically, yes. Mentally, no. Maxine was vaguely aware of another personality, but she said it felt more like someone was watching her, or something was lurking in the shadows. D.I.D. patients often experience lapses of time in which an alter personality takes over. 'Beth' was formed out of necessity to protect Maxine from harm. I believe Beth, as well as several other personalities that have come and gone over the years, were created around the time Maxine was afraid she would never escape the countless years of abuse at the hands of her mother's boyfriend."

Struck with a genuine pang of empathy, I clench my jaw. After everything I read in the social worker's file, I can understand why Maxine's mental health was unstable.

I pride myself on reading suspects and antici-pating their motives. Even though I'm still angry for being duped, I need to give myself some credit. Maxine appeared to be competent in every one of our interviews. Was it possible she was genuinely oblivious to her alter's actions and hadn't known about the evil deeds done by her own hands?

"Based on my intensive sessions with Maxine," Dr. Scanlan continues, "I plan to recommend at her next hearing that she be discharged."

My jaw unhinges. "You're going to suggest that a murderer be released back into society after only a few months of commitment?"

"That's the thing about D.I.D." The doctor releases a long breath while leaning back in her chair. "Only a part of Maxine can be considered accountable for these crimes. I believe with the proper amount of therapy, Beth's homicidal tendencies can be tamed. I've met with her at least a dozen times since Maxine arrived, and she has a cognitive understanding of the situation. She knows what she did was wrong and feels remorse. She allowed Maxine to turn herself in because she agreed it was the right thing to do even though Maxine is innocent of all three murders."

"Hold on." Blinking hard, I shake my head. "I'm sorry, did you say *three*?"

The doctor's thin eyebrows shoot upward. "You weren't made aware of the proceedings in Georgia? I just assumed they would've sent a copy of the court order to the detective involved in her active cases."

Dry, unamused laughter erupts from my lips. "You're saying she killed *another* person in Georgia?"

"Her mother's long-term boyfriend, a man named Martin Clark. The social worker who took Max in believes he'd been molesting Max starting at the age of five. Maxine claimed it was the only way she could finally escape his control. She confessed to the murder just days after her commitment here. Maxine was seventeen at the time of the murder and a victim. The court ruled it to be an act of self-defense."

"And yet you still believe it's okay to let someone mentally ill with violent tendencies walk free?"

"Patients with D.I.D., in general, don't possess violent tendencies. In fact, it's quite rare. I believe because Maxine went untreated for so long, she did everything in her power to hide her condition, including isolating herself from society for nearly a decade. Beth took it upon herself to battle Maxine's demons her own way. She feared that if someone didn't save Maxine, she would self-destruct."

Frustration rattles against my bones. "Yet you have no *hard* evidence that this 'Beth' persona exists."

"I'm basing my diagnosis off a doctorate and decades of experience," the doctor deadpans. A thin smile lifts the corners of her mouth. "Listen, Detective. I could spend *days* educating you on everything I know about this disorder, and it's possible you still wouldn't believe it to be credible. At this point, I'm afraid we'll have to agree to disagree."

"I guess you're right."

The doctor eyes the smartwatch on her wrist. "I'm afraid that's all the time I can spare. The director's on her way to meet with me."

I stand and lean over the desk to shake the doctor's hand. "Thank you for your time, Dr. Scanlan. I hope you're right about Maxine, and there's nothing to worry about regarding her impending release."

Returning to the hallway, I start for the exit until I hear a familiar voice floating from the other direction. I spin around, walking past the small number of open doorways leading to empty patient rooms. At the end of the hallway, a petite blonde sits alone inside a computer lab. On a screen in front of her, a husky woman in an orange jumpsuit twirls her white-blond hair around her finger as she speaks to the camera.

Gabby Gallo.

"...*told* you this would all work out."

"Yeah, only it took a pretty big turn of events," the other woman replies in a Southern drawl. "You goin' to prison wasn't part of the plan." From the flawless texture of the woman's sunshine-yellow hair, I realize she's wearing a wig.

Beth.

Gabby waves a dismissive hand through the air. "I did this to myself. I never should've mentioned my husbands to that detective." With a wistful smile, she sets her elbows on the table before her and rests her chin in her hands. "At least one of us got away with eliminating those causing us pain."

"If I hadn't done somethin', Maxine would've allowed that evil bitch to continue tormentin' her for the rest of her life," Beth agrees. "After her cousin tried to steal every man Maxine cared about, Maxine still had a soft spot for Britta. It's good that she took Roger and Oliver off our hands, though. They were both toxic."

My lips part with a silent gasp. No one had mentioned that Oliver and Maxine had once been an item, or that Britta had an affair with Max's first husband. It's almost understandable why Beth had been so paranoid about Noah's involvement with Britta.

Gabby makes a loud snorting noise. "Seriously. What was her beef with Max?"

"It's complicated." Beth's shoulders rise with a deep inhale. "Britta was angry because her daddy left her momma to be with Maxine's momma."

"Wait a minute. Wasn't it Max's mom's boyfriend who abused Max?"

"Yep," Beth answers, popping the 'p.' "Somehow Britta was convinced both Maxine and her momma seduced her daddy—even though Maxine was only a little girl."

"That's disgusting! I can't believe Max never told me Britta was that sick in the head! I get the heebie-jeebies just thinking about how easily Max's mom or aunt could've stopped poor little Max's nightmare."

Beth glances at the analog clock beyond the monitor. "Listen, I gotta run. Noah's makin' arrangements for us to start house huntin' in Greece as soon as I'm released. I promised I'd narrow it down to a small handful of islands. I only have half an hour before all the psychos return from their outside break and take over the computers."

"Does he think moving across the world will stop you from hooking up with strangers at the bar?"

Beth's shoulders lift. "He claims it's because one of the top D.I.D. experts is located in Athens. Anyway, I promised Maxine that I'd stay loyal to him. Me and her started communicatin' through a diary at the doc's suggestion."

"Either way, I'm jealous you're moving to Greece with the love of your life." Gabby sighs dreamily. "I can't imagine anything more romantic." Then, her eyes spark with excitement. "Promise me you'll find a villa with an extra bedroom so I can visit once that appeal my attorney filed goes through. He says there's an eighty-five percent chance it'll happen before the end of the year."

"It'll happen," Beth agrees. "And we'll celebrate in style once you join us."

As the women say their goodbyes, I whirl around and stomp back to the guard holding my personal effects.

I'll be damned if they're going to realize their dream of celebrating a victory in paradise.

If there's any way to stop either murderous woman from being set free, I vow to make it happen.

Thank you for reading *Right Across the Bay*! If you enjoyed this book, please take a quick minute to leave a review on Amazon, Goodreads, and BookBub. Anything you can do to spread the word about this book is greatly appreciated!

Now available: Detective Josephine Kelly book #2, *Their Little Lies*! Order from Quinn's website: www.quinnavery.com/shop

Want to receive free bonus content, sneak peeks of upcoming releases, and access to my exclusive monthly giveaways? You'll also receive a FREE copy of Quinn's standalone, *What They Never Said*, when you sign up: www.quinnavery.com/subscribe

ACKNOWLEDGMENTS

You'd think remembering who to thank in each book would get easier, but here I am on book #42, knees weak and palms sweaty as I try to think of something clever to say.

First of all, I want to share my gratitude for Najla Qamber and her amazing team. Najla delivered the gorgeous cover I was hoping for and was always right on top of things when I asked for a tweak or update. We've been working together for over a decade now and I can't express how much I love the working relationship we've cultured!

To my #1 fan, Christy Freeberg, thank you for always pushing me to finish when I'm not at my best and encouraging me to keep going! I value our decades-long friendship more than you know—love you more!

Thank you to Corrie Hanson and my mom for always reading the first, wonky drafts and still continuing to cheer me on. You two are the best!

DeDe Kelly, you rock! I'm so glad we met and became friends! I appreciate the pontoon cruises you guys take me on to get me out of the house in the summertime.

To another dear decades-old friend, Heidi Schiltz: thanks for helping me to sound more educated than I am and for always entertaining my wild ideas! Love you, lady! You're the best!

To our neighbors across the bay on Lake Shetek (and other friends in the area, including Molly, Britta, Shelly, Beth, DeDe, and Pete): I hope you're entertained by this story and understand some of your names were solely used in fun and nothing more. Thank you for accepting our friendship with open arms and making us feel at home in the hood. I'm so grateful to have met you all!

Big thank you to my loyal fans, including the librarians and local store owners who faithfully sell my work (especially Alyssa, Becky J., Becki S., and DeDe)! You have no idea how much your support is appreciated!

As always, thank you to my husband and kids for putting up with my BS. I'm one lucky lady to have you all behind me.

ABOUT THE AUTHOR

Quinn Avery is a bestselling author under various pen names of over 45 novels. When not visiting their children all across the country, Quinn and her husband divide their time between their farmstead and lake home in southern Minnesota. Quinn also writes steamy romantic suspense, YA paranormal, middle school fiction, and children's picture books. For more information, visit www.QuinnAvery.com.